REVIEWS FOR A STAB IN THE DARK

"Block knows how to weave a tangled web. And when people try to deceive, which is fairly often in his books, they get into a lot of trouble. Block's plots are taut, and his dialogue realistic without too many embellishments. The characters are tough men and they speak accordingly."

~Rocky Mountain News

"Unusually well written! Block is a deft surgeon, sure and precise. "
~The New York Times

"Riveting...a staggering conclusion. "

~Publishers Weekly

"Convincing suspense. "

~Philadelphia Inquirer

"Block is awfully good, with an ear for dialogue, an eye for low-life types, and a gift for fast and effortless storytelling that bears comparison with Elmore Leonard. "

~Los Angeles Times

REVIEWS FOR
LAWRENCE BLOCK
AND MATTHEW SCUDDER

"When Lawrence Block is in his Matt Scudder mode, crime fiction can sidle up so close to literature that often there's no degree of difference."

~Philadelphia Inquirer

THE
MATTHEW SCUDDER
NOVELS:

AND THE
SHORT STORIES:

A STAB IN THE DARK

A Matthew Scudder Novel

LAWRENCE BLOCK

TELEMACHUS PRESS

This book is a work of fiction. Names, characters, places and incidents are either the product of the author's imagination or are used fictitiously. Any resemblance to actual persons, living or dead, or to actual events or locales is entirely coincidental.

A STAB IN THE DARK

Cover Designed by: Telemachus Press, LLC
Copyright © Thinkstockphotos.com/121176538

Visit the author's websites:
http://www.lawrenceblock.com
http://lawrenceblock.wordpress.com/
Twitter: @LawrenceBlock

Published by Telemachus Press, LLC
http://www.telemachuspress.com

ISBN: 978-1-938135-01-9 (eBook)
ISBN: 978-1-938135-03-3 (EPUB)
ISBN: 978-1-938135-02-6 (Paperback)

Printed in the United States of America

10 9 8 7 6 5 4 3 2 1

FOR PATRICK TRESE

A STAB IN THE DARK

ONE

I didn't see him coming. I was in Armstrong's at my usual table in the rear. The lunch crowd had thinned out and the noise level had dropped. There was classical music on the radio and you could hear it now without straining. It was a gray day out, a mean wind blowing, the air holding a promise of rain. A good day to be stuck in a Ninth Avenue saloon, drinking bourbon-spiked coffee and reading the *Post's* story about some madman slashing passersby on First Avenue.

"Mr. Scudder?"

Sixty or thereabouts. High forehead, rimless eyeglasses over pale blue eyes. Graying blond hair combed to lie flat on the scalp. Say five-nine or -ten. Say a hundred seventy pounds. Light complexion. Cleanshaven. Narrow nose. Small thin-lipped mouth. Gray suit, white shirt, tie striped in red and black and gold. Briefcase in one hand, umbrella in the other.

"May I sit down?"

I nodded at the chair opposite mine. He took it, drew a wallet from his breast pocket and handed me a card. His hands were small and he was wearing a Masonic ring.

I glanced at the card, handed it back. "Sorry," I said.

"But—"

"I don't want any insurance," I said. "And you wouldn't want to sell me any. I'm a bad risk."

He made a sound that might have been nervous laughter. "God," he said. "Of course you'd think that, wouldn't you? I didn't come to sell you anything. I can't remember the last time I wrote an individual policy. My area's group policies for corporations." He placed the card on the blue-checked cloth between us. "Please," he said.

The card identified him as Charles F. London, a general agent with Mutual Life of New Hampshire. The address shown was 42 Pine Street, downtown in the financial district. There were two telephone numbers, one local, the other with a 914 area code. The northern suburbs, that would be. Westchester County, probably.

I was still holding his card when Trina came over to take our order. He asked for Dewar's and soda. I had half a cup of coffee left. When she was out of earshot he said, "Francis Fitzroy recommended you."

"Francis Fitzroy."

"Detective Fitzroy. Thirteenth Precinct."

"Oh, Frank," I said. "I haven't seen him in a while. I didn't even know he was at the Thirteenth now."

"I saw him yesterday afternoon." He took off his glasses, polished their lenses with his napkin. "He recommended you, as I said, and I decided I wanted to sleep on it. I didn't sleep much. I had appointments this morning, and then I went to your hotel, and they said I might find you here."

I waited.

"Do you know who I am, Mr. Scudder?"

"No."

"I'm Barbara Ettinger's father."

"Barbara Ettinger. I don't—wait a minute."

Trina brought his drink, set it down, slipped wordlessly away. His fingers curled around the glass but he didn't lift it from the table.

I said, "The Icepick Prowler. Is that how I know the name?"

"That's right."

"Must have been ten years ago."

"Nine."

"She was one of the victims. I was working over in Brooklyn at the time. The Seventy-eighth Precinct, Bergen and Flatbush. Barbara Ettinger. That was our case, wasn't it?"

"Yes."

I closed my eyes, letting the memory come back. "She was one of the last victims. The fifth or sixth, she must have been."

"The sixth."

"And there were two more after her, and then he went out of business. Barbara Ettinger. She was a schoolteacher. No, but it was something like that. A day-care center. She worked at a day-care center."

"You have a good memory."

"It could be better. I just had the case long enough to determine it was the Icepick Prowler again. At that point we turned it over to whoever had been working that case

all along. Midtown North, I think it was. In fact I think
Frank Fitzroy was at Midtown North at the time."

"That's correct."

I had a sudden rush of sense memory. I remembered
a kitchen in Brooklyn, cooking smells overladen with the
reek of recent death. A young woman lay on the linoleum, her clothing disarrayed, innumerable wounds in
her flesh. I had no memory of what she looked like, only
that she was dead.

I finished my coffee, wishing it were straight bourbon. Across the table from me, Charles London was taking a small tentative sip of his scotch. I looked at the
Masonic symbols on his gold ring and wondered what
they were supposed to mean, and what they meant to
him.

I said, "He killed eight women within a period of a
couple months. Used the same MO throughout, attacked
them in their own homes during daylight hours. Multiple
stab wounds with an icepick. Struck eight times and then
went out of business."

He didn't say anything.

"Then nine years later they catch him. When was it?
Two weeks ago?"

"Almost three weeks."

I hadn't paid too much attention to the newspaper
coverage. A couple of patrolmen on the Upper West Side
had stopped a suspicious character on the streets, and a
frisk turned up an icepick. They took him into the station
house and ran a check on him, and it turned out he was
back on the streets after an extended confinement in
Manhattan State Hospital. Somebody took the trouble to
ask him why he was toting an icepick, and they got lucky
the way you sometimes do. Before anybody knew what

was happening he'd confessed to a whole list of unsolved homicides.

"They ran his picture," I said. "A little guy, wasn't he? I don't remember the name."

"Louis Pinell."

I glanced at him. His hands rested on the table, fingertips just touching, and he was looking down at his hands. I said that he must have been greatly relieved that the man was in custody after all these years.

"No," he said.

The music stopped. The radio announcer hawked subscriptions to a magazine published by the Audubon Society. I sat and waited.

"I almost wish they hadn't caught him," Charles London said.

"Why?"

"Because he didn't kill Barbara."

Later I went back and read all three papers, and there'd been something to the effect that Pinell had confessed to seven Icepick Prowler slayings while maintaining he was innocent of the eighth. If I'd even noted that information first time around, I hadn't paid it any mind. Who knows what a psychotic killer's going to remember nine years after the fact?

According to London, Pinell had more of an alibi than his own memory. The night before Barbara Ettinger was murdered, Pinell had been picked up on the complaint of a counterman at a coffee shop in the east twenties. He was taken to Bellevue for observation, held two days and released. Police and hospital records made it quite clear that he was in a locked ward when Barbara Ettinger was killed.

"I kept trying to tell myself there was a mistake," London said. "A clerk can make a mistake recording an admission or release date. But there was no mistake. And Pinell was very adamant on the subject. He was perfectly willing to admit the other murders. I gather he was proud of them in some way or other. But he was genuinely angry at the idea that a murder he hadn't committed was being attributed to him."

He picked up his glass but put it down without drinking from it. "I gave up years ago," he said. "I took it for granted that Barbara's murderer would never be apprehended. When the series of killings stopped so abruptly, I assumed the killer had either died or moved away. My fantasy was that he'd had a moment of awful clarity, realized what he'd done, and killed himself. It made it easier for me if I was able to believe that, and from what a police officer told me, I gathered that that sort of thing occasionally happens. I came to think of Barbara as having been the victim of a force of nature, as if she'd died in an earthquake or a flood. Her killing was impersonal and her killer unknown and unknowable. Do you see what I mean?"

"I think so."

"Now everything's changed. Barbara wasn't killed by this force of nature. She was murdered by someone who tried to make it look as though her death was the work of the Icepick Prowler. Hers was a very cold and calculating murder." He closed his eyes for a moment and a muscle worked in the side of his face. "For years I thought she'd been killed for no reason at all," he said, "and that was horrible, and now I can see that she was killed for a reason, and that's worse."

"Yes."

"I went to Detective Fitzroy to find out what the police were going to do now. Actually I didn't go to him directly. I went to one place and they sent me to another place. They passed me around, you see, no doubt hoping I'd get discouraged somewhere along the way and leave them alone. I finally wound up with Detective Fitzroy, and he told me that they're not going to do anything about finding Barbara's killer."

"What were you expecting them to do?"

"Reopen the case. Launch an investigation. Fitzroy made me see my expectations were unrealistic. I got angry at first, but he talked me through my anger. He said the case was nine years old. There weren't any leads or suspects then and there certainly aren't any now. Years ago they gave up on all eight of those killings, and the fact that they can close their files on seven of them is simply a gift. It didn't seem to bother him, or any of the officers I talked to, that there's a killer walking around free. I gather that there are a great many murderers walking around free."

"I'm afraid there are."

"But I have a particular interest in this particular murderer." His little hands had tightened up into fists. "She must have been killed by someone who knew her. Someone who came to the funeral, someone who pretended to mourn her. God, I can't stand that!"

I didn't say anything for a few minutes. I caught Trina's eye and ordered a drink. The straight goods this time. I'd had enough coffee for a while. When she brought it I drank off half of it and felt its warmth spread through me, taking some of the chill out of the day.

I said, "What do you want from me?"

"I want you to find out who killed my daughter."

No surprise there. "That's probably impossible," I said.

"I know."

"If there was ever a trail, it's had nine years to go cold. What can I do that the cops can't?"

"You can make an effort. That's something they can't do, or at least it's something they *won't* do, and that amounts to the same thing. I'm not saying they're wrong not to reopen the case. But the thing is that I want them to do it, and I can't do anything about it, but in your case, well, I can hire you."

"Not exactly."

"I beg your pardon?"

"You can't hire me," I explained. "I'm not a private investigator."

"Fitzroy said—"

"They have licenses," I went on. "I don't. They fill out forms, they write reports in triplicate, they submit vouchers for their expenses, they file tax returns, they do all those things and I don't."

"What do you do, Mr. Scudder?"

I shrugged. "Sometimes I'll do a favor for a person," I said, "and sometimes the person will give me some money. As a favor in return."

"I think I understand."

"Do you?" I drank the rest of my drink. I remembered the corpse in that Brooklyn kitchen. White skin, little beads of black blood around the puncture wounds. "You want a killer brought to justice," I said. "You'd better re-alize in front that that's impossible. Even if there's a killer out there, even if there's a way to find out who he is, there's not going to be any evidence lying around after all these years. No bloodstained icepick in somebody's hardware drawer. I could get lucky and come up with a thread, but it won't turn into the kind of thing you can spread out in front of a jury. Somebody killed your daughter and got away with it and it galls you. Won't it be more frustrating if you know who it is and there's nothing you can do about it?"

"I still want to know."

"You might learn things you won't like. You said it yourself—somebody probably killed her for a reason. You might be happier not knowing the reason."

"It's possible."

"But you'll run that risk."

"Yes."

"Well, I guess I can try talking with some people." I got my pen and notebook from my pocket, opened the notebook to a fresh page, uncapped the pen. "I might as well start with you," I said.

We talked for close to an hour and I made a lot of notes. I got another double bourbon and made it last. He had Trina take away his drink and bring him a cup of coffee. She refilled it twice for him before we were finished.

He lived in Hastings-on-Hudson in Westchester County. They'd moved there from the city when Barbara was five and her younger sister Lynn was three. Three years ago, some six years after Barbara's death, London's wife Helen had died of cancer. He lived there alone now, and every once in a while he thought about selling the house, but so far he hadn't gotten around to listing it with a realtor. He supposed it was something he'd do sooner or later, whereupon he'd either move into the city or take a garden apartment somewhere in Westchester.

Barbara had been twenty-six. She'd be thirty-five now if she had lived. No children. She had been a couple of months pregnant when she died, and London hadn't even known that until after her death. Telling me this, his voice broke.

Douglas Ettinger had remarried a couple of years after Barbara's death. He'd been a caseworker for the Welfare Department during their marriage, but he'd quit that job shortly after the murder and gone into sales. His second wife's father owned a sporting goods store on Long Island and after the marriage he'd taken in Ettinger as a partner. Ettinger lived in Mineola with his wife and two or three children—London wasn't sure of the number. He had come alone to Helen London's funeral and London hadn't had any contact with him since then, nor had he ever met the new wife.

Lynn London would be thirty-three in a month. She lived in Chelsea and taught fourth-graders at a progressive private school in the Village. She'd been married shortly after Barbara was killed, and she and her husband had separated after a little over two years of marriage and divorced not long after that. No children.

He mentioned other people. Neighbors, friends. The operator of the day-care center where Barbara had worked. A coworker there. Her closest friend from college. Sometimes he remembered names, sometimes not, but he gave me bits and pieces and I could take it from there. Not that any of it would necessarily lead anywhere.

He went off on tangents a lot. I didn't attempt to rein him in. I thought I might get a better picture of the dead woman by letting him wander, but even so I didn't develop any real sense of her. I learned she was attractive, that she'd been popular as a teenager, that she'd done well in school. She was interested in helping people, she liked working with children, and she'd been eager to have a family of her own. The image that came through was of a woman of no vices and the blandest virtues, wavering in age from childhood to an age she hadn't lived to attain. I had the feeling that he hadn't known her terribly well, that he'd been insulated by his work and by his role as her father from any reliable perception of her as a person.

Not uncommon, that. Most people don't really know their children until the children have become parents themselves. And Barbara hadn't lived that long.

When he ran out of things to tell me I flipped through my notes, then closed the book. I told him I'd see what I could do.

"I'll need some money," I said.

"How much?"

I never know how to set a fee. What's too little and what's too much? I knew I needed money—a chronic condition, that—and that he probably had it in fair supply. Insurance agents can earn a lot or a little, but it seemed to me that selling group coverage to corporations was probably quite lucrative. I flipped a mental coin and came up with a figure of fifteen hundred dollars.

"And what will that buy, Mr. Scudder?"

I told him I really didn't know. "It'll buy my efforts," I said. "I'll work on this until I come up with something or until it's clear to me that there's nothing to come up with. If that happens before I figure I've earned your money you'll get some back. If I feel I have more coming

I'll let you know, and you can decide then whether or not you want to pay me."

"It's very irregular, isn't it?"

"You might not be comfortable with it."

He considered that but didn't say anything. Instead he got out a checkbook and asked how he should make the check payable. To Matthew Scudder, I told him, and he wrote it out and tore it out of the book and set it on the table between us.

I didn't pick it up. I said, "You know, I'm not the only alternative to the police. There are big, well-staffed agencies who operate in a much more conventional manner. They'll report in detail, they'll account for every cent of fees and expenses. On top of that, they've got more resources than I do."

"Detective Fitzroy said as much. He said there were a couple of major agencies he could recommend."

"But he recommended me?"

"Yes."

"Why?" I knew one reason, of course, but it wasn't one he'd have given London.

London smiled for the first time. "He said you're a crazy son of a bitch," he said. "Those were his words, not mine."

"And?"

"He said you might get caught up in this in a way a large agency wouldn't. That when you get your teeth in something you don't let go. He said the odds were against it, but you just might find out who killed Barbara."

"He said that, did he?" I picked up his check, studied it, folded it in half. I said, "Well, he's right. I might."

TWO

It was too late to get to the bank. After London left I settled my tab and cashed a marker at the bar. My first stop
would be the Eighteenth Precinct, and it's considered bad
manners to show up empty-handed.

I called first to make sure he'd be there, then took a
bus east and another one downtown. Armstrong's is on
Ninth Avenue, around the corner from my Fifty-seventh
Street hotel. The Eighteenth is housed on the ground
floor of the Police Academy, a modern eight-story building with classes for recruits and prep courses for the ser-
geants' and lieutenants' exams. They've got a pool there,
and a gym equipped with weight machines and a running track. You can take martial arts courses, or deafen
yourself practicing on the pistol range.

I felt the way I always do when I walk into a station
house. Like an impostor, I suppose, and an unsuccessful
one at that. I stopped at the desk, said I had business
with Detective Fitzroy. The uniformed sergeant waved

me on. He probably assumed I was a member in good standing. I must still look like a cop, or walk like one, or something. People read me that way. Even cops.

I walked on through to the squad room and found Fitzroy typing a report at a corner desk. There were half a dozen Styrofoam coffee cups grouped on the desk, each holding about an inch of light coffee. Fitzroy motioned me to a chair and I sat down while he finished what he was typing. A couple of desks away, two cops were hassling a skinny black kid with eyes like a frog. I gather he'd been picked up for dealing three-card monte. They weren't giving him all that hard of a time, but then it wasn't the crime of the century, either.

Fitzroy looked as I remembered him, maybe a little older and a little heavier. I don't suppose he put in many hours on the running track. He had a beefy Irish face and gray hair cropped close to his skull, and not too many people would have taken him for an accountant or an orchestra conductor or a cabbie. Or a stenographer—he made pretty good time on his typewriter, but he only used two fingers to do it.

He finished finally and pushed the machine to one side. "I swear the whole thing's paperwork," he said. "That and court appearances. Who's got time left to detect anything? Hey, Matt." We shook hands. "Been a while. You don't look so bad."

"Was I supposed to?"

"No, course not. How about some coffee? Milk and sugar?"

"Black is fine."

He crossed the room to the coffee machine and came back with another pair of Styrofoam cups. The two detectives went on ragging the three-card dealer, telling him they figured he had to be the First Avenue Slasher. The kid kept up his end of the banter reasonably well.

Fitzroy sat down, blew on his coffee, took a sip, made a face. He lit a cigarette and leaned back in his swivel chair. "This London," he said. "You saw him?"

"Just a little while ago."

"What did you think? You gonna help him out?"

"I don't know if that's the word for it. I told him I'd give it a shot."

"Yeah, I figured there might be something in it for you, Matt. Here's a guy looking to spend a few dollars. You know what it's like, it's like his daughter up and died all over again and he's got to think he's doing something about it. Now there's nothing he *can* do, but if he spends a few dollars he'll maybe feel better, and why shouldn't it go to a good man who can use it? He's got a couple bucks, you know. It's not like you're taking it from a crippled newsie."

"That's what I gathered."

"So you'll give it a shot," he said. "That's good. He wanted me to recommend somebody to him and right off I thought of you. Why not give the business to a friend, right? People take care of each other and that makes the world go on spinning. Isn't that what they say?"

I had palmed five twenties while he was getting the coffee. Now I leaned forward and tucked them into his hand. "Well, I can use a couple days work," I said. "I appreciate it."

"Listen, a friend's a friend, right?" He made the money disappear. A friend's a friend, all right, but a favor's a favor and there are no free lunches, not in or out of the department. And why should there be? "So you'll chase around and ask a few questions," he went on, "and you can string him for as long as he wants to play, and you don't have to bust your hump over it. Nine years, for Christ's sake. Wrap this one up and we'll fly you down to Dallas, let you figure out who killed JFK."

"It must be a pretty cold trail."

"Colder'n Kelsey's legendary nuts. If there was any reason at the time to think she wasn't just one more entry in the Icepick Prowler's datebook, then maybe somebody would of done a little digging at the time. But you know how those things work."

"Sure."

"We got this guy now over here on First Avenue taking whacks at people on the street, swinging at 'em with a butcher knife. We got to figure they're random attacks, right? You don't run up to the victim's husband and ask him was she fucking the mailman. Same with what's-her-name, Ettinger. Maybe she *was* fucking the mailman and maybe that's why she got killed, but there didn't look to be any reason to check it out at the time and it's gonna be a neat trick to do it now."

"Well, I can go through the motions."

"Sure, why not?" He tapped an accordion-pleated manila file. "I had them pull this for you. Why don't you do a little light reading for a few minutes? There's a guy I gotta see."

He was gone a little better than half an hour. I spent the time reading my way through the Icepick Prowler file. Early on, the two detectives popped the three-card dealer into a holding cell and rushed out, evidently to run down a tip on the First Avenue Slasher. The Slasher had done his little number right there in the Eighteenth, just a couple of blocks from the station house, and they were evidently pretty anxious to put him away.

I was done with the file when Frank Fitzroy got back. He said, "Well? Get anything?"

"Not a whole lot. I made a few notes. Mostly names and addresses."

"They may not match up after nine years. People move. Their whole fucking lives change."

God knows mine did. Nine years ago I was a detective on the NYPD. I lived on Long Island in a house with a lawn and a backyard and a barbecue grill and a wife and two sons. I had moved, all right, though it was sometimes difficult to determine the direction. Surely my life had changed.

I tapped the file folder. "Pinell," I said. "How sure is it he didn't kill Barbara Ettinger?"

"Gilt-edged, Matt. Bottled in bond. He was in Bellevue at the time."

"People have been known to slip in and out."

"Granted, but he was in a straitjacket. That hampers your movement a little. Besides, there's things that set the Ettinger killing apart from the others. You only notice them if you look for them, but they're there."

"Like what?"

"Number of wounds. Ettinger had the lowest number of wounds of all eight victims. The difference isn't major but maybe it's enough to be significant. Plus all the other victims had wounds in the thighs. Ettinger had nothing in the thighs or legs, no punctures. Thing is, there was a certain amount of variation among the other victims. He didn't stamp out these murders with a cookie cutter. So the discrepancies with Ettinger didn't stand out at the time. The fewer wounds and the no wounds in the thighs, you can look at it that he was rushed, he heard somebody or thought he heard somebody and he didn't have time to give her the full treatment."

"Sure."

"The thing that made it so obvious that it was the Icepick guy who cooled her, well, you know what that was."

"The eyes."

"Right." He nodded approval. "All of the victims were stabbed through the eyes. One shot through each eyeball. That never made the papers. We held it back the way you always try and hold one or two things back to keep the psychos from fooling you with false confessions. You wouldn't believe how many clowns already turned themselves in for the slashings down the street."

"I can imagine."

"And you have to check 'em all out, and then you have to write up each interrogation, and that's the real pain in the ass. Anyway, getting back to Ettinger. The Icepick guy always went for the eyes. We kept the wraps on that detail, and Ettinger got it in the eye, so what are you going to figure? Who's gonna give a shit if she got it in the thighs or not when you've got an eyeball puncture to run with?"

"But it was only one eye."

"Right. Okay, that's a discrepancy, but it lines up with the fewer punctures and the no wounds in the thighs. He's in a hurry. No time to do it right. Wouldn't you figure it that way?"

"Anybody would."

"Of course. You want some more coffee?"

"No thanks."

"I guess I'll pass myself. I've had too much already today."

"How do you figure it now, Frank?"

"Ettinger? What do I figure happened?"

"Uh-huh."

He scratched his head. Vertical frown lines creased his forehead on either side of his nose. "I don't think it was anything complicated," he said. "I think somebody read the papers and watched television and got turned on by the stories about the Icepick guy. You get these imitators every now and then. They're psychos without the imagination to think up their own numbers so they hitch a ride on somebody else's craziness. Some loony watched the six o'clock news and went out and bought an icepick."

"And happened to get her in the eye by chance?"

"Possible. Could be. Or it could be it just struck him as a good idea, same as it did Pinell. Or something leaked."

"That's what I was thinking."

"Far as I can remember, there was nothing in the papers or on the news. Nothing about the eye wounds, I mean. But maybe there was and then we squelched it but not before this psycho read it or heard it and it made an impression. Or maybe it never got into the media but the word was around. You got a few hundred cops who know something, plus everybody who's around for the postmortems, plus everybody who sees the records, all the clerks and all, and each of them tells three people and those people all talk, and how long does it take before a lot of people know about it?"

"I see what you mean."

"If anything, the business with the eyes makes it look like it was just a psycho. A guy who tried it once for a thrill and then let it go."

"How do you figure that, Frank?"

He leaned back, interlaced his fingers behind his head. "Well, say it's the husband," he said. "Say he wants to kill her because she's fucking the mailman, and he wants to make it look like the Icepick Prowler so he won't carry the can for it himself. If he knows about the eyes, he's gonna do both of them, right? He's not taking any chances. A nut, he's something else again. He does one eye because it's something to do, and then maybe he's bored with it so he doesn't do the other one. Who knows what goes through their fucking heads?"

"If it's a psycho, then there's no way to tag him."

"Of course there isn't. Nine years later and you're looking for a killer without a motive? That's a needle in a haystack when the needle's not even there. But that's all right. You take this and play with it, and after you've run the string you just tell London it must have been a psycho. Believe me, he'll be happy to hear it."

"Why?"

"Because that's what he thought nine years ago, and he got used to the idea. He accepted it. Now he's afraid it's somebody he knows and that's driving him crazy, so you'll investigate it all for him and tell him everything's okay, the sun still comes up in the east every morning and his daughter was still killed by a fucking Act of God. He can relax again and go back to his life. He'll get his money's worth."

"You're probably right."

"'Course I'm right. You could even save yourself running around and just sit on your ass for a week and then tell him what you'll wind up telling him anyway. But I don't suppose you'll do that, will you?"

"No, I'll give it my best shot."

"I figured you'd at least go through the motions. What it is, you're still a cop, aren't you, Matt?"

"I suppose so. In a way. Whatever that means."

"You don't have anything steady, huh? You just catch a piece of work like this when it comes along?"

"Right."

"You ever think about coming back?"

"To the department? Not very often. And never very seriously."

He hesitated. There were questions he wanted to ask, things he wanted to say to me, but he decided to leave them unsaid. I was grateful for that. He got to his feet and so did I. I thanked him for the time and the information and he said an old friend was an old friend and it was a pleasure to be able to help a pal out. Neither of us mentioned the hundred dollars that had changed hands. Why should we? He'd been glad to get it and I was glad to give it. A favor's no good unless you pay for it. One way or the other, you always do.

THREE

It had rained a little while I was with Fitzroy. It wasn't raining when I got back outside, but it didn't feel as though it was through for the day. I had a drink around the corner on Third Avenue and watched part of the newscast. They showed the police artist's sketch of the Slasher, the same drawing that was on the front page of the *Post*. It showed a round-faced black man with a trimmed beard and a cap on his head. Mad zeal glinted in his large almond-shaped eyes.

"Imagine that comin' up the street at you," the bartender said. "I'll tell you, there's a lot of guys gettin' pistol permits on the strength of this one. I'm thinkin' about fillin' out an application myself."

I remember the day I stopped carrying a gun. It was the same day I turned in my shield. I'd had a stretch of feeling terribly vulnerable without that iron on my hip, and now I could hardly recall how it had felt to walk around armed in the first place.

I finished my drink and left. Would the bartender get a gun? Probably not. More people talked about it than did it. But whenever there's the right kind of nut making headlines, a Slasher or an Icepick Prowler, a certain number of people get pistol permits and a certain number of others buy illegal guns. Then some of them get drunk and shoot their wives. None of them ever seems to wind up nailing the Slasher.

I walked uptown, stopped at an Italian place along the way for dinner, then spent a couple of hours at the main library on Forty-second Street, dividing my time between old newspapers on microfilm and new and old Polk city directories. I made some notes, but not many. I was mostly trying to let myself sink into the case, to take a few steps backward in time.

By the time I got out of there it was raining. I took a cab to Armstrong's, got a stool at the bar and settled in. There were people to talk to and bourbon to drink, with enough coffee to keep fatigue at bay. I didn't hit it very hard, just coasted along, getting by, getting through. You'd be surprised what a person can get through.

The next day was Friday. I read a paper with breakfast. There'd been no slashings the previous night, but neither had there been any progress in the case. In Ecuador, a few hundred people had died in an earthquake. There seemed to be more of those lately, or I was more aware of them.

I went to my bank, put Charles London's check in my savings account, drew out some cash and a money order for five hundred dollars. They gave me an envelope to go with the money order and I addressed it to Ms. Anita

Scudder in Syosset. I stood at the counter for a few minutes with the bank's pen in my hand, trying to think of a note to include, and wound up sending the money order all by itself. After I'd mailed it I thought about calling to tell her it was in the mail, but that seemed like even more of a chore than thinking of something to put in a note.

It wasn't a bad day. Clouds obscured the sun, but there were patches of blue overhead and the air had a tang to it. I stopped at Armstrong's to cover my marker and left without having anything. It was a little early for the day's first drink. I left, walked east a long block to Columbus Circle, and caught a train.

I rode the D to Smith and Bergen and came out into sunshine. For a while I walked around, trying to get my bearings. The Seventy-eighth Precinct, where I'd served a brief hitch, was only six or seven blocks to the east, but that had been a long time ago and I'd spent little time in Brooklyn since. Nothing looked even faintly familiar. I was in a part of the borough that hadn't had a name until fairly recently. Now a part of it was called Cobble Hill and another chunk was called Boerum Hill and both of them were participating wholeheartedly in the brownstone renaissance.

Neighborhoods don't seem to stand still in New York. They either improve or deteriorate. Most of the city seemed to be crumbling. The whole South Bronx was block after block of burned-out buildings, and in Brooklyn the same process was eroding Bushwick and Brownsville.

These blocks were going in the other direction. I walked up one street and down another and found myself becoming aware of changes. There were trees on every block, most of them planted within the past few years. While some of the brownstones and brickfronts were in disrepair, more sported freshly painted trim. The shops reflected the changes that had been going on. A health food store on Smith Street, a boutique at the corner of Warren and Bond, little up-scale restaurants tucked in all over the place.

The building where Barbara Ettinger had lived and died was on Wyckoff Street between Nevins and Bond. It was a brick tenement, five stories tall with four small apartments on each floor, and it had thus escaped the conversion that had already turned many of the brownstones back into the one-family houses they had originally been. Still, the building had been spruced up some. I stood in the vestibule and checked the names on the mailboxes, comparing them to those I'd copied from an old city directory. Of the twenty apartments, only six held tenants who'd been there at the time of the murder.

Except you can't go by names on mailboxes. People get married or unmarried and their names change. An apartment gets sublet to keep the landlord from raising the rent, and the name of a long-dead tenant stays on the lease and on the mailbox for ages. A roommate moves in, then stays on when the original leaseholder moves out. There are no shortcuts. You have to knock on all the doors.

I rang a bell, got buzzed in, went to the top floor and worked my way down. It's a little easier when you have a badge to flash but the manner's more important than the ID, and I couldn't lose the manner if I tried. I didn't tell anyone I was a cop, but neither did I try to keep anyone from making the assumption.

The first person I talked to was a young mother in one of the rear apartments on the top floor. Her baby cried in the next room while we talked. She'd moved in within the past year, she told me, and she didn't know anything about a murder nine years previously. She asked anxiously if it had taken place in that very apartment, and seemed at once relieved and disappointed to learn it had not.

A Slavic woman, her hands liver-spotted and twisted with arthritis, gave me a cup of coffee in her fourth-floor front apartment. She put me on the couch and turned her own chair to face me. It had been positioned so she could watch the street.

She'd been in that apartment for almost forty years, she told me. Up until four years ago her husband had been there, but now he was gone and she was alone. The neighborhood, she said, was getting better. "But the old people are going. Places I shopped for years are gone. And the price of everything! I don't believe the prices."

She remembered the icepick murder, though she was surprised it had been nine years. It didn't seem that long to her. The woman who was killed was a nice woman, she said. "Only nice people get killed."

She didn't seem to remember much about Barbara Ettinger beyond her niceness. She didn't know if she had been especially friendly or unfriendly with any of the other neighbors, if she'd gotten on well or poorly with her husband. I wondered if she even remembered what the woman had looked like, and wished I had a picture to show her. I might have asked London for one if I'd thought of it.

Another woman on the fourth floor, a Miss Wicker, was the only person to ask for identification. I told her I wasn't a policeman, and she left the chain lock on the door and spoke to me through a two-inch opening, which didn't strike me as unreasonable. She'd only been in the building a few years, did know about the murder and that the Icepick Prowler had been recently apprehended, but that was the extent of her information.

"People let anyone in," she said. "We have an intercom here but people just buzz you in without determining who you are. People talk about crime but they never believe it can happen to them, and then it does." I thought of telling her how easy it would be to snap her chain lock with a bolt cutter, but I decided her anxiety level was high enough already.

A lot of the tenants were out for the day. On the third floor, Barbara Ettinger's floor, I got no response from one of the rear apartments, then paused in front of the adjoining door. The pulse of disco music came through it. I knocked, and after a moment the door was opened by a man in his late twenties. He had short hair and a mustache, and he was wearing nothing but a pair of blue-striped white gym shorts. His body was well-muscled, and his tanned skin glistened with a light coating of sweat.

I told him my name and that I'd like to ask him a few questions. He led me inside, closed the door, then moved past me and crossed the room to the radio. He lowered the volume about halfway, paused, turned it off altogether.

There was a large mat in the center of the uncarpeted parquet floor. A barbell and a pair of dumbbells reposed on it, and a jump rope lay curled on the floor alongside. "I was just working out," he said. "Won't you sit down? That chair's the comfortable one. The other's nice to visit but you wouldn't want to live there."

I took the chair while he sat on the mat and folded his legs tailor-fashion. His eyes brightened with recognition when I mentioned the murder in 3-A. "Donald told me," he said. "I've only been here a little over a year but Donald's been living here for ages. He's watched the neighborhood become positively chic around him. Fortunately this particular building retains its essential tackiness. You'll probably want to talk to Donald but he won't be home from work until six or six thirty."

"What's Donald's last name?"

"Gilman." He spelled it. "And I'm Rolfe Waggoner. That's Rolfe with an e. I was just reading about the Icepick Prowler. Of course I don't remember the case. I was in high school then. That was back home in Indiana—Muncie, Indiana—and that was a long ways from here." He thought for a moment. "In more ways than one," he said.

"Was Mr. Gilman friendly with the Ettingers?"

"He could answer that better than I can. You've caught the man who did it, haven't you? I read that he was in a mental hospital for years and nobody ever knew he killed anybody, and then he was released and they caught him and he confessed or something?"

"Something like that."

"And now you want to make sure you have a good case against him." He smiled. He had a nice open face and he seemed quite at ease, sitting on a mat in his gym shorts. Gay men used to be so much more defensive, especially around cops. "It must be complicated with something that happened so many years ago. Have you talked with Judy? Judy Fairborn, she's in the apartment where the Ettingers used to live. She works nights, she's a waitress, so she'll be home now unless she's at an audition or a dance class or shopping or—well, she'll be home unless she's out, but that's always the case, isn't it?" He smiled again, showing me perfectly even teeth. "But maybe you've already spoken with her."

"Not yet."

"She's new. I think she moved in about six months ago. Would you want to talk to her anyway?"

"Yes."

He uncoiled, sprang lightly to his feet. "I'll introduce you," he said. "Just let me put some clothes on. I won't be a minute."

He reappeared wearing jeans and a flannel shirt and running shoes without socks. We crossed the hall and he knocked on the door of Apartment 3-A. There was silence, then footsteps and a woman's voice asking who it was.

"Just Rolfe," he said. "In the company of a policeman who'd like to grill you, Ms. Fairborn."

"Huh?" she said, and opened the door. She might have been Rolfe's sister, with the same light brown hair, the same regular features, the same open Midwestern countenance. She wore jeans, too, and a sweater and penny loafers. Rolfe introduced us and she stepped aside and motioned us in. She didn't know anything about the Ettingers, and her knowledge of the murder was limited to the fact that it had taken place there. "I'm glad I didn't know before I moved in," she said, "because I might have let it spook me, and that would have been silly, wouldn't it? Apartments are too hard to find. Who can afford to be superstitious?"

"Nobody," Rolfe said. "Not in this market."

They talked about the First Avenue Slasher, and about a recent wave of local burglaries, including one a week ago on the first floor. I asked if I could have a look at the kitchen. I was on my way there as I asked the question. I think I'd have remembered the layout anyway, but I'd already been in other apartments in the building and they were all the same.

Judy said, "Is this where it happened? Here in the kitchen?"

"Where did you think?" Rolfe asked her. "The bedroom?"

"I guess I didn't think about it."

"You didn't even wonder? Sounds like repression."

"Maybe."

I tuned out their conversation. I tried to remember the room, tried to peel off nine years and be there once again, standing over Barbara Ettinger's body. She'd been near the stove then, her legs extending into the center of the small room, her head turned toward the living room. There had been linoleum on the floor and that was gone, the original wood floor restored and glossy with polyurethane. And the stove looked new, and plaster had been removed to expose the brick exterior wall. I couldn't be sure the brick hadn't been exposed previously, nor could I know how much of my mental picture was real. The memory is a cooperative animal, eager to please; what it cannot supply it occasionally invents, sketching carefully to fill in the blanks.

Why the kitchen? The door led into the living room, and she'd let him in either because she knew who he was or in spite of the fact that she didn't, and then what? He drew the icepick and she tried to get away from him? Caught her heel in the linoleum and went sprawling, and then he was on her with the pick?

The kitchen was the middle room, separating the living room and bedroom. Maybe he was a lover and they were on their way to bed when he surprised her with a few inches of pointed steel. But wouldn't he wait until they got where they were going?

Maybe she had something on the stove. Maybe she was fixing him a cup of coffee. The kitchen was too small to eat in but more than large enough for two people to stand comfortably waiting for water to boil.

Then a hand over her mouth to muffle her cries and a thrust into her heart to kill her. Then enough other thrusts of the icepick to make it look like the Icepick Prowler's work.

Had the first wound killed her? I remembered beads of blood. Dead bodies don't bleed freely, but neither do most puncture wounds. The autopsy had indicated a wound in the heart that had been more or less instantly fatal. It might have been the first wound inflicted or the last, for all I'd seen in the Medical Examiner's report.

Judy Fairborn filled a teakettle, lit the stove with a wooden match, and poured three cups of instant coffee when the water boiled. I'd have liked bourbon in mine, or instead of mine, but nobody suggested it. We carried our cups into the living room and she said, "You looked as though you saw a ghost. No, I'm wrong. You looked as though you were looking for one."

"Maybe that's what I was doing."

"I'm not sure if I believe in them or not. They're supposed to be more common in cases of sudden death when the victim didn't expect what happened. The theory is that the soul doesn't realize it died, so it hangs around because it doesn't know to pass on to the next plane of existence."

"I thought it walked the floors crying out for vengeance," Rolfe said. "You know, dragging chains, making the boards creak."

"No, it just doesn't know any better. What you do, you get somebody to lay the ghost."

"I'm not going to touch that line," Rolfe said.

"I'm proud of you. You get high marks for restraint. That's what it's called, laying the ghost. It's a sort of exorcism. The ghost expert, or whatever you call him, communicates with the ghost and lets him know what happened, and that he's supposed to pass on. And then the spirit can go wherever spirits go."

"You really believe all this?"

"I'm not sure what I believe," she said. She uncrossed her legs, then recrossed them. "If Barbara's haunting this apartment, she's being very restrained about it. No creaking boards, no midnight apparitions."

"Your basic low-profile ghost," he said.

"I'll have nightmares tonight," she said. "If I sleep at all."

I knocked on all the doors on the two lower floors without getting much response. The tenants were either out or had nothing useful to tell me. The building's superintendent had a basement apartment in a similar building on the next block, but I didn't see the point in looking him up. He'd only been on the job for a matter of months, and the old woman in the fourth-floor-front apartment had told me there had been four or five supers in the past nine years.

By the time I got out of the building I was glad for the fresh air, glad to be on the street again. I'd felt something in Judy Fairborn's kitchen, though I wouldn't go so far as to call it a ghost. But it had felt as though something from years past was pulling at me, trying to drag me down and under.

Whether it was Barbara Ettinger's past or my own was something I couldn't say.

I stopped at a bar on the corner of Dean and Smith. They had sandwiches and a microwave oven to heat them in but I wasn't hungry. I had a quick drink and sipped a short beer chaser. The bartender sat on a high stool drinking a large glass of what looked like vodka. The other two customers, black men about my age, were at the far end of the bar watching a game show on TV. From time to time one of them was talking back to the set.

I flipped a few pages in my notebook, went to the phone and looked through the Brooklyn book. The day-care center where Barbara Ettinger had worked didn't seem to be in business. I checked the Yellow Pages to see if there was anything listed under another name at the same address. There wasn't.

The address was on Clinton Street, and I'd been away from the neighborhood long enough so that I had to ask directions, but once I'd done so it was only a walk of a few blocks. The boundaries of Brooklyn neighborhoods aren't usually too well defined—the neighborhoods themselves are often largely the invention of realtors—but when I crossed Court Street I was leaving Boerum Hill for Cobble Hill, and the change wasn't difficult to see. Cobble Hill was a shade or two tonier. More trees, a higher percentage of brownstones, a greater proportion of white faces on the street.

I found the number I was seeking on Clinton between Pacific and Amity. There was no day-care center there. The ground floor storefront offered supplies for knitting and needlepoint. The proprietor, a plump Earth Mother with a gold incisor, didn't know anything about a day-care center. She'd moved in a year and a half ago after a health food restaurant had gone out of business. "I ate there once," she said, "and they *deserved* to go out of business. Believe me."

She gave me the landlord's name and number. I tried him from the corner and kept getting a busy signal so I walked over to Court Street and climbed a flight of stairs. There was just one person in the office, a young man with his sleeves rolled up and a large round ashtray full of cigarette butts on the desk in front of him. He chain-smoked while he talked on the phone. The windows were closed and the room was as thick with smoke as a nightclub at four in the morning.

When he got off the phone I caught him before it could ring again. His own memory went back beyond the health food restaurant to a children's clothing store that had also failed in the same location. "Now we got needlepoint," he said. "If I were gonna guess I'd say she'll be out in another year. How much can you make selling yarn? What happens, somebody has a hobby, an interest, so they open up a business. Health food, needlepoint, whatever it is, but they don't know shit about business and they're down and out in a year or two. She breaks the lease, we'll rent it in a month for twice what she pays. It's a renter's market in an upscale neighborhood." He reached for the phone. "Sorry I can't help you," he said.

"Check your records," I said.

He told me he had lots of important things to do, but halfway through the statement changed from an assertion to a whine. I sat in an old oak swivel chair and let him fumble around in his files. He opened and closed half a dozen drawers before he came up with a folder and slapped it down on his desk.

"Here we go," he said. "Happy Hours Child Care Center. Some name, huh?"

"What's wrong with it?"

"Happy hour's in a bar when the drinks are half price. Hell of a thing to call a place for the kiddies, don't you think?" He shook his head. "Then they wonder why they go out of business."

I didn't see anything the matter with the name.

"Leaseholder was a Mrs. Corwin. Janice Corwin. Took the place on a five-year lease, gave it up after four years. Quit the premises eight years ago in March." That would have been a year after Barbara Ettinger's death. "Jesus, you look at the rent and you can't believe it. You know what she was paying?"

I shook my head.

"Well, you saw the place. Name a figure." I looked at him. He stubbed out a cigarette and lit another. "One and a quarter. Hundred and twenty-five dollars a month. Goes for six now and it's going up the minute the needlework lady goes out, or when her lease is up. Whichever comes first."

"You have a forwarding address for Corwin?"

He shook his head. "I got a residential address. Want it?" He read off a number on Wyckoff Street. It was just a few doors from the Ettingers' building. I wrote down the address. He read off a phone number and I jotted that down, too.

His phone rang. He picked it up, said hello, listened for a few minutes, then talked in monosyllables. "Listen, I got someone here," he said after a moment. "I'll get back to you in a minute, okay?"

He hung up and asked me if that was all. I couldn't think of anything else. He hefted the file. "Four years she had the place," he said. "Most places drop dead in the first year. Make it through a year you got a chance. Get through two years and you got a good chance. You know what's the problem?"

"What?"

"Women," he said. "They're amateurs. They got no need to make a go of it. They open a business like they try on a dress. Take it off if they don't like the color. If that does it, I got calls to make."

I thanked him for his help.

"Listen," he said, "I always cooperate. It's my nature."

I tried the number he gave me and got a woman who spoke Spanish. She didn't know anything about anybody named Janice Corwin and didn't stay on the line long enough for me to ask her much of anything. I dropped another dime and dialed again on the chance that I'd misdialed the first time. When the same woman answered I broke the connection.

When they disconnect a phone it's close to a year before they reassign the number. Of course Mrs. Corwin could have changed her number without moving from the Wyckoff Street address. People, especially women, do that frequently enough to shake off obscene callers.

Still, I figured she'd moved. I figured everyone had moved, out of Brooklyn, out of the five boroughs, out of the state. I started to walk back toward Wyckoff Street, covered half a block, turned, retraced my steps, started to turn again.

I made myself stop. I had an anxious sensation in my chest and stomach. I was blaming myself for wasting time and starting to wonder why I'd taken London's check in the first place. His daughter was nine years in the grave, and whoever killed her had probably long since started a brand-new life in Australia. All I was doing was spinning my goddamned wheels.

I stood there until the intensity of the feeling wound itself down, knowing that I didn't want to go back to Wyckoff Street. I'd go there later, when Donald Gilman got home from work, and I could check Corwin's address then. Until then I couldn't think of anything I felt like doing about the Ettinger murder. But there was something I could do about the anxiety.

One thing about Brooklyn—you never have to walk very far before you encounter a church. They're all over the place throughout the borough.

The one I found was at the corner of Court and Congress. The church itself was closed and the iron gate locked, but a sign directed me to St. Elizabeth Seton's Chapel right around the corner. A gateway led to a one-story chapel tucked in between the church and the rectory. I walked through an ivy-planted courtyard which a plaque proclaimed to be the burial site of Cornelius Heeney. I didn't bother reading who he was or why they'd planted him there. I walked between rows of white statues and into the little chapel. The only other person in it was a frail Irishwoman kneeling in a front pew. I took a seat toward the back.

It's hard to remember just when I started hanging out in churches. It happened sometime after I left the force, sometime after I moved out of the house in Syosset and away from Anita and the boys and into a hotel on West Fifty-seventh. I guess I found them to be citadels of peace and quiet, two commodities hard to come by in New York.

I sat in this one for fifteen or twenty minutes. It was peaceful, and just sitting there I lost some of what I'd been feeling earlier.

Before I left I counted out a hundred fifty dollars, and on my way out I slipped the money into a slot marked "For the Poor." I started tithing not long after I began spending odd moments in churches, and I don't know why I started or why I've never stopped. The question doesn't plague me much. There is no end of things I do without knowing the reason why.

I don't know what they do with the money. I don't much care. Charles London had given me fifteen hundred dollars, an act which didn't seem to make much more sense than my passing on a tenth of that sum to the unspecified poor.

There was a shelf of votive candles, and I stopped to light a couple of them. One for Barbara London Ettinger, who had been dead a long time, if not so long as old Cornelius Heeney. Another for Estrellita Rivera, a little girl who had been dead almost as long as Barbara Ettinger.

I didn't say any prayers. I never do.

FOUR

Donald Gilman was twelve or fifteen years older than his roommate, and I don't suppose he put in as many hours with the dumbbells and the jump rope. His neatly combed hair was a sandy brown, his eyes a cool blue through heavy horn-rimmed glasses. He was wearing suit pants and a white shirt and tie. His suit jacket was draped over the chair Rolfe had warned me about.

Rolfe had said Gilman was a lawyer, so I wasn't surprised when he asked to see my identification. I explained that I had resigned from the police force some years earlier. He raised an eyebrow at this news and flicked a glance at Rolfe.

"I'm involved in this at the request of Barbara Ettinger's father," I went on. "He's asked me to investigate."

"But why? The killer's been caught, hasn't he?"

"There's some question about that."

"Oh?"

I told him that Louis Pinell had an unbreakable alibi for the day of Barbara Ettinger's murder.

"Then someone else killed her," he said at once. "Unless the alibi turns out to be unfounded. That would explain the father's interest, wouldn't it? He probably suspects—well, he could suspect anyone at all. I hope you won't take it amiss if I call him to confirm that you're here as his emissary?"

"He may be hard to reach." I had kept London's card and I got it out of my wallet. "He's probably left the office by now, and I wouldn't think he's arrived home yet. He lives alone, his wife died a couple years ago, so he most likely takes his meals at restaurants."

Gilman looked at the card for a moment, then handed it back. I watched his face and could see him make up his mind. "Oh, well," he said. "I can't see the harm in talking with you, Mr. Scudder. It's not as though I knew anything substantial. It was all a fair amount of years ago, wasn't it? A lot of water under the bridge since then, or over the dam, or wherever it goes." His blue eyes brightened. "Speaking of liquid, we generally have a drink about now. Will you join us?"

"Thank you."

"We generally mix up some martinis. Unless there's something else you'd prefer?"

"Martinis hit me a little hard," I said. "I think I'd better stick with whiskey. Bourbon, if you've got it."

Of course they had it. They had Wild Turkey, which is a cut or two better than what I'm used to, and Rolfe gave me five or six ounces of it in a cut-crystal Old Fashioned glass. He poured Bombay gin into a pitcher, added ice cubes and a spoonful of vermouth, stirred gently and strained the blend into a pair of glasses that were mates to mine. Donald Gilman raised his glass and proposed a toast to Friday, and we drank to that.

I wound up sitting where Rolfe had had me sit earlier. Rolfe sat as before on the rug, his knees drawn up and his arms locked around them. He was still wearing the jeans and shirt he'd put on to introduce me to Judy Fairborn. His weights and jump rope were out of sight. Gilman sat on the edge of the uncomfortable chair and leaned forward, looking down into his glass, then looking up at me.

"I was trying to remember the day she died," he said. "It's difficult. I didn't come home from the office that day. I had drinks with someone after work, and then dinner out, and I think I went to a party in the Village. It's not important. The point is that I didn't get home until the following morning. I knew what to expect when I got here because I read the morning paper with my breakfast. No, that's wrong. I remember that I bought the *News* because it's easier to manage on the train, the business of turning the pages and all. The headline was *Icepick Killer Strikes in Brooklyn,* or words to that effect. I believe there had been a previous killing in Brooklyn."

"The fourth victim. In Sheepshead Bay."

"Then I turned to page three, I suppose it must have been, and there was the story. No photograph, but the name and address, of course, and that was unmistakable." He put a hand to his chest. "I remember how I felt. It was incredibly shocking. You don't expect that sort of thing to happen to someone you know. And it made me feel so vulnerable myself, you know. It happened in this building. I felt that before I felt the sense of loss one feels over the death of a friend."

"How well did you know the Ettingers?"

"Reasonably well. They were a couple, of course, and most of their social interaction was with other couples. But they were right across the hall and I'd have them in for drinks or coffee from time to time, or they'd ask me over. I had one or two parties that they came to, but they didn't stay very long. I think they were comfortable enough with gay people, but not in great quantity. I can understand that. One doesn't like to be overwhelmingly outnumbered, does one? It's only natural to feel self-conscious."

"Were they happy?"

The question pulled him back to the Ettingers and he frowned, weighing his answer. "I suppose he's a suspect," he said. "The spouse always is. Have you met him?"

"No."

"'Were they happy?' The question's inevitable, but who can ever answer it? They seemed happy. Most couples do, and most couples ultimately break up, and when they do their friends are invariably surprised because they *seemed* so bloody happy." He finished his drink. "I think they were happy enough. She was expecting a child when she was killed."

"I know."

"I hadn't known it. I only learned after her death." He made a little circle with the empty glass, and Rolfe got gracefully to his feet and replenished Gilman's drink. While he was up he poured me another Wild Turkey. I was feeling the first one a little bit so I took it easy on the second.

Gilman said, "I thought it might have steadied her."

"The baby?"

"Yes."

"She needed steadying?"

He sipped his martini. "*De mortuis* and all that. One hesitates to speak candidly of the dead. There was a restlessness in Barbara. She was a bright girl, you know. Very attractive, energetic, quick-witted. I don't recall where she went to school, but it was a good school. Doug went to Hofstra. I don't suppose there's anything the matter with Hofstra, but it's less prestigious than Barbara's alma mater. I don't know why I can't remember it."

"Wellesley." London had told me.

"Of course. I'd have remembered. I dated a Wellesley girl during my own college career. Sometimes self-acceptance takes a certain amount of time."

"Did Barbara marry beneath herself?"

"I wouldn't say that. On the surface, she grew up in Westchester and went to Wellesley and married a social worker who grew up in Queens and went to Hofstra. But a lot of that is just a matter of labels." He took a sip of gin. "She may have thought she was too good for him, though."

"Was she seeing anybody else?"

"You do ask direct questions, don't you? It's not hard to believe you were a policeman. What made you leave the force?"

"Personal reasons. Was she having an affair?"

"There's nothing tackier than dishing the dead, is there? I used to hear them sometimes. She would accuse him of having sex with women he met on the job. He was a welfare caseworker and that involved visiting unattached women in their apartments, and if one's in the market for casual sex the opportunity's certainly there. I don't know that he was taking advantage of it, but he struck me as the sort of man who would. And I gather she thought he was."

"And she was having an affair to get even?"

"Quick of you. Yes, I think so, but don't ask me with whom because I've no idea. I would sometimes be home during the day. Not often, but now and then. There were times when I heard her coming up the stairs with a man, or I might pass her door and hear a man's voice. You have to understand that I'm not a busybody, so I didn't try to catch a peek of the mystery man, whoever he was. In fact I didn't pay the whole business a great deal of attention."

"She would entertain this man during the day?"

"I can't swear she was entertaining anybody. Maybe it was the plumber come to repair a leaky faucet. Please understand that. I just had the feeling that she might have been seeing someone, and I knew she had accused her husband of infidelity, so I thought she might be getting a bit of sauce for the goose."

"But it was during the day. Didn't she work days?"

"Oh, at the day-care center. I gather her schedule was quite flexible. She took the job to have something to do. Restlessness, again. She was a psychology major and she'd been in graduate school but gave it up, and now she wasn't doing anything, so she started helping out at the day-care center. I don't think they paid her very much and I don't suppose they objected if she took the odd afternoon off."

"Who were her friends?"

"God. I met people at their apartment but I can't remember any of them. I think most of their friends were his friends. There was the woman from the day-care center, but I'm afraid I don't remember her name."

"Janice Corwin."

"Is that it? It doesn't even ring a muted bell. She lived nearby. Just across the street, if I'm right."

"You are. Do you know if she's still there?"

"No idea. I can't remember when I saw her last. I don't know that I'd recognize her anyway. I think I met her once, but I may just recall her because Barbara talked about her. You say the name was Corwin?"

"Janice Corwin."

"The day-care center's gone. It closed years ago."

"I know."

The conversation didn't go much further. They had a dinner date and I'd run out of questions to ask. And I was feeling the drinks. I'd finished the second one without being aware of it and was surprised when I found the glass empty. I didn't feel drunk but I didn't feel sober either, and my mind could have been clearer.

The cold air helped. There was a wind blowing. I hunched my shoulders against it and walked across the street and down the block to the address I had for Janice Corwin. It turned out to be a four-story brick building, and a few years back someone had bought it, turned out the tenants as soon as their leases expired, and converted it for single-family occupancy.

According to the owner, whose name I didn't bother catching, the conversion process was still going on. "It's endless," he said. "Everything's three times as difficult as you figure, takes four times as long, and costs five times as much. And those are conservative figures. Do you know how long it takes to strip old paint off door jambs?

Do you know how many doorways there are in a house like this?"

He didn't remember the names of the tenants he'd dispossessed. The name Janice Corwin was not familiar to him. He said he probably had a list of the tenants somewhere but he didn't even know where to start looking for it. Besides, it wouldn't have their forwarding addresses. I told him not to bother looking.

I walked to Atlantic Avenue. Among the antique shops with their Victorian oak furniture and the plant stores and the Middle Eastern restaurants I managed to find an ordinary coffee shop with a Formica counter and red leatherette stools. I wanted a drink more than I wanted a meal, but I knew I'd be in trouble if I didn't have something to eat. I had Salisbury steak and mashed potatoes and green beans and made myself eat everything. It wasn't bad. I drank two cups of so-so coffee and paused on my way out to look up Corwin in the phone book. There were two dozen Corwins in Brooklyn, including a J. Corwin with an address that looked to be in Bay Ridge or Bensonhurst. I tried the number but nobody answered.

No reason to think she'd be in Brooklyn. No reason to think she'd be listed under her own name, and I didn't know her husband's name.

No point checking the post office. They don't hold address changes longer than a year, and the building on Wyckoff Street had changed hands longer ago than that. But there would be ways to trace the Corwins. There generally are.

I paid the check and left a tip. According to the counterman, the nearest subway was a couple blocks away on Fulton Street. I was on the train heading for Manhattan

before I realized that I hadn't even bothered to walk over
to Bergen and Flatbush and take a look at the station
house of the Seventy-eighth Precinct. Somehow I hadn't
thought of it.

FIVE

I stopped at the desk when I got back to my hotel. No mail, no messages. Upstairs in my room I cracked the seal on a bottle of bourbon and poured a few fingers into a glass. I sat there for a while skipping around in a paperback edition of *The Lives of the Saints*. The martyrs held a curious fascination for me. They'd found such a rich variety of ways of dying.

Couple of days earlier there'd been an item in the paper, a back-pages squib about a suspect arrested for the year-old murder of two women in their East Harlem apartment. The victims, a mother and daughter, had been found in their bedroom, each with a bullet behind the ear. The report said the cops had stayed on the case because of the unusual brutality of the murders. Now they'd made an arrest, taking a fourteen-year-old boy into custody. He'd have been thirteen when the women were killed.

According to the story's last paragraph, five other persons had been killed in or around the victims' build-

ing in the year since their murder. There'd been no indi-
cation whether those five murders were solved, or
whether the kid in custody was suspected of them.

I let my mind slip off on tangents. Now and again I'd
put the book aside and find myself thinking about Barbara Ettinger. Donald Gilman had started to say that her
father probably suspected someone, then caught himself
and left the name unsaid.

The husband, probably. The spouse is always the first
suspect. If Barbara hadn't apparently been one of a series
of victims, Douglas Ettinger would have been grilled six
ways and backwards. As it was, he'd been interrogated
automatically by detectives from Midtown North. They
could hardly have done otherwise. He was not only the
husband. He was also the person who had discovered the
body, coming upon her corpse in the kitchen upon returning from work.

I'd read a report of the interrogation. The man who
conducted it had already taken it for granted that the killing was the work of the Icepick Prowler, so his questions
had concentrated on Barbara's schedule, on her possible
propensity for opening the door for strangers, on
whether she might have mentioned anyone following her
or behaving suspiciously. Had she been bothered recently by obscene telephone calls? People hanging up
without speaking? Suspicious wrong numbers?

The questioning had essentially assumed the subject's
innocence, and the assumption had certainly been logical
enough at the time. Evidently there had been nothing in
Douglas Ettinger's manner to arouse suspicion.

I tried, not for the first time, to summon up a memory
of Ettinger. It seemed to me that I must have met him.
We were on the scene before Midtown North came to

take the case away from us, and he'd have had to be somewhere around while I was standing in that kitchen eyeing the body sprawled on the linoleum. I might have tried to offer a word of comfort, might have formed some impression, but I couldn't remember him at all.

Perhaps he'd been in the bedroom when I was there, talking with another detective or with one of the patrolmen who'd been first on the scene. Maybe I'd never laid eyes on him, or maybe we'd spoken and I'd forgotten him altogether. I had by that time spent quite a few years seeing any number of recently bereaved. They couldn't all stand out in sharp relief in the cluttered warehouse of memory.

Well, I'd see him soon enough. My client hadn't said whom he suspected, and I hadn't asked, but it stood to reason that Barbara's husband headed the list. London wouldn't be all that upset by the possibility that she'd died at the hands of someone he didn't even know, some friend or lover who meant nothing to him. But for her to have been killed by her own husband, a man London knew, a man who had been present years later at London's wife's funeral—

There's a phone in my room but the calls go through the switchboard, and it's a nuisance placing them that way even when I don't care if the operator listens in. I went down to the lobby and dialed my client's number in Hastings. He answered on the third ring.

"Scudder," I said. "I could use a picture of your daughter. Anything as long as it's a good likeness."

"I took albums full of pictures. But most of them were of Barbara as a child. You would want a late photograph, I suppose?"

"As late as possible. How about a wedding picture?"

"Oh," he said. "Of course. There's a very good picture of the two of them, it's in a silver frame on a table in the living room. I suppose I could have it copied. Do you want me to do that?"

"If it's not too much trouble."

He asked if he should mail it and I suggested he bring it to his office Monday. I said I'd call and arrange to pick it up. He asked if I'd had a chance to begin the investigation yet and I told him I'd spent the day in Brooklyn. I tried him on a couple of names—Donald Gilman, Janice Corwin. Neither meant anything to him. He asked, tentatively, if I had any leads.

"It's a pretty cold trail," I said.

I rang off without asking him who he suspected. I felt restless and went around the corner to Armstrong's. On the way I wished I'd taken the time to go back to my room for my coat. It was colder, and the wind had an edge to it.

I sat at the bar with a couple of nurses from Roosevelt. One of them, Terry, was just finishing up her third week in Pediatrics. "I thought I'd like the duty," she said, "but I can't stand it. Little kids, it's so much worse when you lose one. Some of them are so brave it breaks your heart. I can't handle it, I really can't."

Estrellita Rivera's image flashed in my mind and was gone. I didn't try to hold onto it. The other nurse, glass in hand, was saying that all in all she thought she preferred Sambuca to Amaretto. Or maybe it was the other way around.

I made it an early night.

SIX

Even if I couldn't recall meeting Douglas Ettinger, I had a picture of him in my mind. Tall and raw-boned, dark hair, pallid skin, knobby wrists, Lincolnesque features. A prominent Adam's apple.

I woke up Saturday morning with his image firmly in mind, as if it had been imprinted there during an unremembered dream. After a quick breakfast I went down to Penn Station and caught a Long Island Railroad local to Hicksville. A phone call to his house in Mineola had established that Ettinger was working at the Hicksville store, and it turned out to be a $2.25 cab ride from the station.

In an aisle lined with squash and racquet-ball equipment I asked a clerk if Mr. Ettinger was in. "I'm Doug Ettinger," he said. "What can I do for you?"

He was about five-eight, a chunky one-seventy. Tightly curled light brown hair with red highlights. The plump cheeks and alert brown eyes of a squirrel. Large

white teeth, with the upper incisors slightly bucked, con-
sistent with the squirrel image. He didn't look remotely
familiar, nor did he bear any resemblance whatsoever to
the rail-splitter caricature I'd dreamed up to play his
part.

"My name's Scudder," I said. "I'd like to talk to you
privately, if you don't mind. It's about your wife."

His open face turned guarded. "Karen?" he said.
"What about her?"

Christ. "Your first wife."

"Oh, Barbara," he said. "You had me going for a second there. The serious tone and all, and wanting to talk
to me about my wife. I don't know what I thought.
You're from the NYPD? Right this way, we can talk in
the office."

His was the smaller of the two desks in the office. In-
voices and correspondence were arranged in neat piles
on it. A Lucite photo cube held pictures of a woman and
several young children. He saw me looking at it and said,
"That's Karen there. And the kids."

I picked up the cube, looked at a young woman with
short blonde hair and a sunny smile. She was posed next
to a car, with an expanse of lawn behind her. The whole
effect was very suburban.

I replaced the photo cube and took the chair Ettinger
indicated. He sat behind the desk, lit a cigarette with a
disposable butane lighter. He knew the Icepick Prowler
had been apprehended, knew too that the suspect denied
any involvement in his first wife's murder. He assumed
Pinell was lying, either out of memory failure or for some
insane reason. When I explained that Pinellas's alibi had
been confirmed, he seemed unimpressed.

"It's been years," he said. "People can get mixed up on dates and you never know how accurate records are. He probably did it. I wouldn't take his word that he didn't."

"The alibi looks sound."

Ettinger shrugged. "You'd be a better judge of that than I would. Still, I'm surprised that you guys are reopening the case. What can you expect to accomplish after all this time?"

"I'm not with the police, Mr. Ettinger."

"I thought you said—"

"I didn't bother to correct your impression. I used to be in the department. I'm private now."

"You're working for somebody?"

"For your former father-in-law."

"Charlie London hired you?" He frowned, taking it all in. "Well, I guess it's his privilege. It's not going to bring Barbie back but I guess it's his right to feel like he's doing something. I remember he was talking about posting a reward after she was murdered. I don't know if he ever got around to it or not."

"I don't believe he did."

"So now he wants to spend a few dollars finding the real killer. Well, why not? He doesn't have much going for him since Helen died. His wife, Barbara's mother."

"I know."

"Maybe it'll do him good to have something he can take an interest in. Not that work doesn't keep him busy, but, well—" He flicked ashes from his cigarette. "I don't know what help I can give you, Mr. Scudder, but ask all the questions you want."

I asked about Barbara's social contacts, her relationships with people in the building. I asked about her job at the day-care center. He remembered Janice Corwin but couldn't supply her husband's name. "The job wasn't that important," he said. "Basically it was something to get her out of the house, give her a focus for her energy. Oh, the money helped. I was dragging a briefcase around for the Welfare Department, which wasn't exactly the road to riches. But Barbie's job was temporary. She was going to give it up and stay home with the baby."

The door opened. A teenage clerk started to enter the office, then stopped and stood there looking awkward. "I'll be a few minutes, Sandy," Ettinger told him. "I'm busy right now."

The boy withdrew, shutting the door. "Saturday's always busy for us," Ettinger said. "I don't want to rush you, but I'm needed out there."

I asked him some more questions. His memory wasn't very good, and I could understand why. He'd had one life torn up and had had to create a new one, and it was easier to do so if he dwelled on the first life as little as possible. There were no children from that first union to tie him into relations with in-laws. He could leave his marriage to Barbara in Brooklyn, along with his case-worker's files and all the trappings of that life. He lived in the suburbs now and drove a car and mowed a lawn and lived with his kids and his blonde wife. Why sit around remembering a tenement apartment in Boerum Hill?

"Funny," he said. "I can't begin to think of anyone we knew who might be capable of...of doing what was done to Barbie. But one other thing I could never believe was that she'd let a stranger into the apartment."

"She was careful about that sort of thing?"

"She was always on guard. Wyckoff Street wasn't the kind of neighborhood she grew up in, although she found it comfortable enough. Of course we weren't going to stay there forever." His glance flicked to the photo cube, as if to picture Barbara standing next to a car and in front of a lawn. "But she got spooked by the other icepick killings."

"Oh?"

"Not at first. When he killed the woman in Sheepshead Bay, though, that's when it got to her. Because it was the first time he'd struck in Brooklyn, you see. It freaked her a little."

"Because of the location? Sheepshead Bay's a long ways from Boerum Hill."

"But it was Brooklyn. And there was something else, I think, because I remember she identified pretty strongly with the woman who got killed. I must have known why but I can't remember. Anyway, she got nervous. She told me she had the feeling she was being watched."

"Did you mention that to the police?"

"I don't think so." He lowered his eyes, lit another cigarette. "I'm sure I didn't. I thought at the time that it was part of being pregnant. Like craving odd foods, that sort of thing. Pregnant women get fixated on strange things." His eyes rose to meet mine. "Besides, I didn't want to think about it. Just a day or two before the murder she was talking about how she wanted me to get a police lock for the door. You know those locks with a steel bar braced against the door so it can't be forced?"

I nodded.

"Well, we didn't get a lock like that. Not that it would have made any difference because the door wasn't forced. I wondered why she would let anyone in, as nervous as she was, but it was daytime, after all, and people aren't as suspicious in the daytime. A man could pretend to be a plumber or from the gas company or something. Isn't that how the Boston Strangler operated?"

"I think it was something like that."

"But if it was actually someone she knew—"

"There are some questions I have to ask."

"Sure."

"Is it possible your wife was involved with anyone?"

"Involved with—you mean having an affair?"

"That sort of thing."

"She was pregnant," he said, as if that answered the question. When I didn't say anything he said, "We were very happy together. I'm sure she wasn't seeing anyone."

"Did she often have visitors when you were out?"

"She might have had a friend over. I didn't check up on her. We trusted each other."

"She left her job early that day."

"She did that sometimes. She had an easygoing relationship with the woman she worked for."

"You said you trusted each other. Did she trust you?"

"What are you driving at?"

"Did she ever accuse you of having affairs with other women?"

"Jesus, who've you been talking to? Oh, I bet I know where this is coming from. Sure. We had a couple of arguments that somebody must have heard."

"Oh?"

"I told you women get odd ideas when they're pregnant. Like food cravings. Barbie got it into her head that I was making it with some of my cases. I was dragging my ass through tenements in Harlem and the South Bronx, filling out forms and trying not to gag on the smell and dodging the crap they throw off the roof at you, and she was accusing me of getting it on with all of those damsels in distress. I came to think of it as a pregnancy neurosis. I'm not Mr. Irresistible in the first place, and I was so turned off by what I saw in those hovels that I had trouble performing at home some of the time, let alone being turned on while I was on the job. The hell, you were a cop, I don't have to tell you the kind of thing I saw every day."

"So you weren't having an affair?"

"Didn't I just tell you that?"

"And you weren't romancing anybody else? A woman in the neighborhood, for example?"

"Certainly not. Did somebody say I was?"

I ignored the question. "You remarried about three years after your wife died, Mr. Ettinger. Is that right?"

"A little less than three years."

"When did you meet your present wife?"

"About a year before I married her. Maybe more than that, maybe fourteen months. It was in the spring, and we had a June wedding."

"How did you meet?"

"Mutual friends. We were at a party, although we didn't pay any attention to each other at the time, and then a friend of mine had both of us over for dinner, and—" He broke off abruptly. "She wasn't one of my ADC cases in the South Bronx, if that's what you're getting at. And she never lived in Brooklyn, either. Jesus, I'm stupid!"

"Mr. Ettinger—"

"I'm a suspect, aren't I? Jesus, how could I sit here and not have it occur to me? I'm a suspect, for Christ's sake."

"There's a routine I have to follow in order to pursue an investigation, Mr. Ettinger."

"Does he think I did it? London? Is that what this whole thing is about?"

"Mr. London hasn't told me who he does or doesn't suspect. If he's got any specific suspicions, he's keeping them to himself."

"Well, isn't that decent of him." He ran a hand over his forehead. "Are we about through now, Scudder? I told you we're busy on Saturdays. We get a lot of people who work hard all week and Saturday's when they want to think about sports. So if I've answered all your questions—"

"You arrived home about six-thirty the day your wife was murdered."

"That sounds about right. I'm sure it's in a police report somewhere."

"Can you account for your time that afternoon?"

He stared at me. "We're talking about something that happened nine years ago," he said. "I can't distinguish one day of knocking on doors from another. Do you remember what *you* did that afternoon?"

"No, but it was a less significant day in my life. You'd remember if you took any time away from your work."

"I didn't. I spent the whole day working on my cases. And it was whatever time I said it was when I got back to Brooklyn. Six-thirty sounds about right." He wiped his forehead again. "But you can't ask me to prove any of this, can you? I probably filed a report but they only keep those things for a few years. I forget whether it's three years or five years, but it's certainly not nine years. Those files get cleaned out on a regular basis."

"I'm not asking for proof."

"I didn't kill her, for God's sake. Look at me. Do I look like a killer?"

"I don't know what killers look like. I was just reading the other day about a thirteen-year-old boy who shot two women behind the ear. I don't know what he looks like, and I don't imagine he looks like a killer." I took a blank memo slip from his desk, wrote a number on it. "This is my hotel," I said. "You might think of something. You never know what you might remember."

"I don't want to remember anything."

I got to my feet. So did he.

"That's not my life anymore," he said. "I live in the suburbs and I sell skis and sweat suits. I went to Helen's funeral because I couldn't think of a decent way to skip it. I should have skipped it. I—"

I said, "Take it easy, Ettinger. You're angry and you're scared but you don't have to be either one. Of course you're a suspect. Who would investigate a woman's murder without checking out the husband? When's the last time you heard of an investigation like that?" I put a hand on his shoulder. "Somebody killed her," I said, "and it may have been somebody she knew. I probably won't be able to find out much of anything but I'm giving it my best shot. If you think of anything, call me. That's all."

"You're right," he said. "I got angry. I—"

I told him to forget it. I found my own way out.

SEVEN

I read a paper on the train ride back to the city. A feature article discussed the upturn in muggings and suggested ways for the reader to make himself a less attractive target. Walk in pairs and groups, the reporter advised. Stick to well-lighted streets. Walk near the curb, not close to buildings. Move quickly and give an impression of alertness. Avoid confrontations. Muggers want to size you up and see if you'll be easy. They ask you the time, ask for directions. Don't let them take advantage of you.

It's wonderful how the quality of urban life keeps getting better. *"Pardon me, sir, but could you tell me how to get to the Empire State Building?"* *"Fuck off, you creep."* Manners for a modern city.

The train took forever. It always felt a little strange going out to Long Island. Hicksville was nowhere near where Anita and the boys lived but Long Island is Long Island and I got the vaguely uncomfortable feeling I always get when I go there. I was glad to get back to Penn Station.

By then it was time for a drink, and I had a quick one in a commuters' bar right there in the station. Saturday might be a busy day for Douglas Ettinger but it was a slow one for the bartender at the Iron Horse. All his weekday customers must have been out in Hicksville buying pup tents and basketball shoes.

The sun was out when I hit the street. I walked across Thirty-fourth, then headed up Fifth to the library. Nobody asked me what time it was, or how to get to the Holland Tunnel.

Before I went into the library I stopped at a pay phone and called Lynn London. Her father had given me her number and I checked my notebook and dialed it. I got an answering machine with a message that began by repeating the last four digits of the number, announced that no one could come to the phone, and invited me to leave my name. The voice was female, very precise, just the slightest bit nasal, and I supposed it belonged to Barbara's sister. I rang off without leaving a message.

In the library I got the same Polk directory for Brooklyn that I'd used earlier. This time I looked up a different building on Wyckoff Street. It had held four apartments then, and one of them had been rented to a Mr. and Mrs. Edward Corwin.

That gave me a way to spend the afternoon. In a bar on Forty-first and Madison I ordered a cup of coffee and a shot of bourbon to pour into it and changed a dollar into dimes. I started on the Manhattan book, where I found two Edward Corwins, an E. Corwin, an E. J. Cor-

win and an E. V. Corwin. When none of those panned
out I used Directory Assistance, getting the Brooklyn list-
ings first, then moving on to Queens, the Bronx and
Staten Island. Some of the numbers I dialed were busy,
and I had to try them four or five times before I got
through. Others didn't answer.

I wound up getting more dimes and trying all the J.
Corwins in the five boroughs. Somewhere in the course
of this I had a second cup of coffee with a second shot of
bourbon in it. I used up quite a few dimes to no discerni-
ble purpose, but most investigatory work is like that. If
she just roots around enough, even a blind sow gets an
acorn now and then. Or so they tell me.

By the time I left the bar, some two-thirds of my
phone numbers had check marks next to them indicating
I'd reached the party and he or she was not the Corwin I
was looking for. I'd call the rest of them in due course if I
had to, but I didn't feel very hopeful about them. Janice
Corwin had closed a business and given up an apartment. She might have moved to Seattle while she was at
it. Or she and her husband could be somewhere in Westchester or Jersey or Connecticut, or out in Hicksville pric-
ing tennis rackets. There was a limit to how much
walking my fingers could do, in the white or yellow
pages.

I went back to the library. I knew when she'd closed
up shop at the Happy Hours Child Care Center; I'd
learned that much from her landlord. Had she and her
husband moved out of Boerum Hill at about the same
time?

I worked year by year through the Polk directories
and found the year the Corwins dropped out of the brick
building on Wyckoff Street. The timing was right. She

had probably closed the day-care center as a prelude to moving. Maybe they'd gone to the suburbs, or his company transferred him to Atlanta. Or they split up and went separate ways.

I put the directory back, then got an intelligent thought for a change and went back to reclaim it. There were three other tenants in the building who'd remained there for a few years after the Corwins moved out. I copied their names in my notebook.

This time I made my calls from a bar on Forty-second Street, and I bypassed the Manhattan book and went straight to Brooklyn information. I got lucky right away with the Gordon Pomerances, who had stayed in Brooklyn when the Wyckoff Street building was sold out from under them. They'd moved a short mile to Carroll Street.

Mrs. Pomerance answered the phone. I gave my name and said I was trying to reach the Corwins. She knew at once who I was talking about but had no idea how I could reach them.

"We didn't keep in touch. He was a nice fellow, Eddie, and he used to bring the children over for dinner after she moved out, but then when he moved we lost contact. It's been so many years. I'm sure we had his address at one point but I can't even remember the city he moved to. It was in California, I think Southern California."

"But she moved out first?"

"You didn't know that? She left him, left him flat with the two kids. She closed the whatchamacallit, the day-care center, and the next thing you know he's got to find a day-care center for his own children. I'm sorry, but I can't imagine a mother walking out on her own children."

"Do you know where she might have gone?"

"Greenwich Village, I suppose. To pursue her art. Among other things."

"Her art?"

"She fancied herself a sculptor. I never saw her work so for all I know she may have had some talent. I'd be surprised if she did, though. There was a woman who had everything. A nice apartment, a husband who was an awfully sweet guy, two beautiful children, and she even had a business that wasn't doing too badly. And she walked away from it, turned her back and walked away."

I tried a long shot. "Did you happen to know a friend of hers named Barbara Ettinger?"

"I didn't know her that well. What was that name? Ettinger? Why is that name familiar to me?"

"A Barbara Ettinger was murdered down the block from where you lived."

"Just before we moved in. Of course. I remember now. I never knew her, naturally, because as I said it was just before we moved in. She was a friend of the Corwins?"

"She worked for Mrs. Corwin."

"Were they that way?"

"What way?"

"There was a lot of talk about the murder. It made me nervous about moving in. My husband and I told each other we didn't have to worry about lightning striking twice in the same place, but privately I was still worried. Then those killings just stopped, didn't they?"

"Yes. You never knew the Ettingers?"

"No, I told you."

An artist in Greenwich Village. A sculptor. Of the J. Corwins I'd been unable to reach, had any lived in the Village? I didn't think so.

I said, "Would you happen to remember Mrs. Corwin's maiden name?"

"Remember it? I don't think I ever knew it in the first place. Why?"

"I was thinking she might have resumed it if she's pursuing an artistic career."

"I'm sure she did. Artistic career or not, she'd want her own name back. But I couldn't tell you what it was."

"Of course she could have remarried by now—"

"Oh, I wouldn't count on it."

"I beg your pardon?"

"I don't think she remarried," Mrs. Pomerance said. There was a sharpness to her tone and I wondered at it. I asked her what made her say that.

"Put it this way," she said. "Sculpture or no sculpture, she'd probably live in Greenwich Village."

"I don't understand."

"You don't?" She clicked her tongue, impatient with my obtuseness. "She left her husband—*and* two children—but not to run off with another man. She left him for another woman."

Janice Corwin's maiden name was Keane. It took a subway ride to Chambers Street and a couple of hours in various offices of the Department of Records and Information Services to supply this kernel of information. Most of the time was spent getting clearance. I kept needing the permission of someone who didn't come in on Saturdays.

I tried marriage licenses first, and when that failed to pan out I had a shot at birth certificates. Mrs. Pomerance had been a little hazy on the names and ages of the Corwin children, but she was pretty sure the youngest's name was Kelly and that she'd been five or six when her mother left. She'd been seven, it turned out; she'd be around fifteen now. Her father was Edward Francis Corwin, her mother the former Janice Elizabeth Keane.

I wrote the name in my notebook with a sense of triumph. Not that there was much likelihood that it would slip my mind, but as a symbol of accomplishment. I couldn't prove that I was an inch closer to Barbara Ettinger's killer than I'd been when Charles London sat down across from me at Armstrong's, but I'd done some detecting and it felt good. It was plodding work, generally pointless work, but it let me use muscles I didn't get to use all that often and they tingled from the exertion.

A couple of blocks from there I found a Blarney Stone with a steam table. I had a hot pastrami sandwich and drank a beer or two with it. There was a big color set mounted over the bar. It was tuned to one of those sports anthology shows they have on Saturday afternoons. A couple of guys were doing something with logs in a fast-moving stream. Riding them, I think. Nobody in the place was paying much attention to their efforts. By the time I was done with my sandwich the log-riders were through and a stock car race had replaced them. Nobody paid any attention to the stock cars, either.

I called Lynn London again. This time when her machine picked up I waited for the beep and left my name and number. Then I checked the phone book.

No Janice Keanes in Manhattan. Half a dozen Keanes with the initial J. Plenty of other variations of the name—

Keene, Keen, Kean. I thought of that old radio show, *Mr. Keene, Tracer of Lost Persons*. I couldn't remember how he spelled it.

I tried all the J. Keanes. I got two that failed to answer, one persistent busy signal, and three people who denied knowing a Janice Keane. The busy signal lived on East Seventy–third Street and I decided that was no address for a lesbian sculptor from Boerum Hill. I dialed Directory Assistance, all set to go through my routine again for the other four boroughs, but something stopped me.

She was in Manhattan. Damn it, I knew she was in Manhattan.

I asked for a Janice Keane in Manhattan, spelled the last name, waited a minute, and was told the only listing in Manhattan under that name and with that spelling was unpublished. I hung up, called back again to get a different operator, and went through the little ritual that a cop uses to obtain an unlisted number. I identified myself as Detective Francis Fitzroy, of the Eighteenth Precinct. I called it the One-Eight Precinct because, although cops don't invariably talk that way, civilians invariably think they do.

I got the address while I was at it. She was on Lispenard Street, and that was a perfectly logical place for a sculptor to be living, and not too long a walk from where I was.

I had another dime in my hand. I put it back in my pocket and went back to the bar. The stock cars had given way to the feature of the program, a couple of black junior–middleweights topping a fight card in some unlikely place. Phoenix, I think it was. I don't know what a junior-middleweight is. They've added all these intermediate weight classes so that they can have more cham-

pionship fights. Some of the patrons who'd passed up the
log-rollers and the stock cars were watching these two
boys hit each other, which was something they weren't
doing very often. I sat through a few rounds and drank
some coffee with bourbon in it.

Because I thought it would help if I had some idea
how I was going to approach this woman. I'd been track-
ing her spoor through books and files and phone wires,
as if she held the secret to the Ettinger murder, and for all
I knew Barbara Ettinger was nothing to her beyond a
faceless lump who put the alphabet blocks away when
the kids were done playing with them.

Or she was Barbara's best friend. Or her lover—I remembered Mrs. Pomerance's questions: "She was a
friend of the Corwins? Were they that way?"

Maybe she had killed Barbara. Could they have both
left the day–care center early? Was that even possible, let
alone likely?

I was spinning my wheels and I knew it but I let them
spin for a while anyway. On the television screen, the kid
with the white stripe on his trunks was finally beginning
to use his jab to set up right hands to the body. It didn't
look as though he was going to take his man out in the
handful of rounds remaining, not like that, but he
seemed a safe shot for the decision. He was wearing his
opponent down, grinding away at him. Jabbing with the
left, hooking the right hand to the rib section. The other
boy couldn't seem to find a defense that worked.

I knew how both of them felt.

I thought about Douglas Ettinger. I decided he didn't
kill his wife, and I tried to figure out how I knew that,
and decided I knew it the same way I'd known Janice

Keane was in Manhattan. Chalk it up to divine inspiration.

Ettinger was right, I decided. Louis Pinell killed Barbara Ettinger, just as he'd killed the other seven women. Barbara had thought some nut was stalking her and she was right.

Then why'd she let the nut into her apartment?

In the tenth round, the kid who'd been getting his ribs barbecued summoned up some reserve of strength and put a couple of combinations together. He had the kid with the stripe on his trunks reeling, but the flurry wasn't enough to end it and the kid with the stripe hung on and got the decision. The crowd booed. I don't know what fight they thought they were watching. The crowd in Phoenix, that is. My companions in the Blarney Stone weren't that involved emotionally.

The hell with it. I went and made my phone call.

It rang four or five times before she answered it. I said, "Janice Keane, please," and she said she was Janice Keane.

I said, "My name's Matthew Scudder, Ms. Keane. I'd like to ask you some questions."

"Oh?"

"About a woman named Barbara Ettinger."

"Jesus." A pause. "What about her?"

"I'm investigating her death. I'd like to come over and talk with you."

"You're investigating her death? That was ages ago. It must have been ten years."

"Nine years."

"I thought it was the Mounties who never gave up. I never heard that about New York's Finest. You're a policeman?"

I was about to say yes, but heard myself say, "I used to be."

"What are you now?"

"A private citizen. I'm working for Charles London. Mrs. Ettinger's father."

"That's right, her maiden name was London." She had a good telephone voice, low-pitched and throaty. "I can't make out why you're starting an investigation now. And what could I possibly contribute to it?"

"Maybe I could explain that in person," I said. "I'm just a few minutes away from you now. Would it be all right if I come over?"

"Jesus. What's today, Saturday? And what time is it? I've been working and I tend to lose track of the time. I've got six o'clock. Is that right?"

"That's right."

"I'd better fix something to eat. And I have to clean up. Give me an hour, okay?"

"I'll be there at seven."

"You know the address?" I read it off as I'd received it from Information. "That's it. That's between Church and Broadway, and you ring the bell and then stand at the curb so I can see you and I'll throw the key down. Ring two long and three short, okay?"

"Two long and three short."

"Then I'll know it's you. Not that you're anything to me but a voice on the phone. How'd you get this number? It's supposed to be unlisted."

"I used to be a cop."

"Right, so you said. So much for unlisted numbers, huh? Tell me your name again."

"Matthew Scudder."

She repeated it. Then she said, "Barbara Ettinger. Oh, if you knew how that name takes me back. I have a feeling I'm going to be sorry I answered the phone. Well, Mr. Scudder, I'll be seeing you in an hour."

EIGHT

Lispenard is a block below Canal Street, which puts it in
that section known as Tribeca. Tribeca is a geographical
acronym for Triangle Below Canal, just as SoHo derives
from South of Houston Street. There was a time when
artists began moving into the blocks south of the Village,
living in violation of the housing code in spacious and
inexpensive lofts. The code had since been modified to
permit residential loft dwelling and SoHo had turned
chic and expensive, which led loft seekers further south
of Tribeca. The rents aren't cheap there either now, but
the streets still have the deserted quality of SoHo ten or
twelve years ago.

I stuck to a well-lighted street. I walked near the curb,
not close to buildings, and I did my best to move quickly
and give an impression of alertness. Confrontations were
easily avoided in those empty streets.

Janice Keane's address turned out to be a six-story loft
building, a narrow structure fitted in between two taller,

wider and more modern buildings. It looked cramped, like a little man on a crowded subway. Floor-to-ceiling windows ran the width of the facade on each of its floors. On the ground floor, shuttered for the weekend, was a wholesaler of plumber's supplies.

I went into a claustrophobic hallway, found a bell marked Keane, rang it two long and three short. I went out to the sidewalk, stood at the curb looking up at all those windows.

She called down from one of them, asking my name. I couldn't see anything in that light. I gave my name, and something small whistled down through the air and jangled on the pavement beside me. "Fifth floor," she said. "There's an elevator."

There was indeed, and it could have accommodated a grand piano. I rode it to the fifth floor and stepped out into a spacious loft. There were a lot of plants, all deep green and thriving, and relatively little in the way of furniture. The doors were oak, buffed to a high sheen. The walls were exposed brick. Overhead track lighting provided illumination.

She said, "You're right on time. The place is a mess but I won't apologize. There's coffee."

"If it's no trouble."

"None at all. I'm going to have a cup myself. Just let me steer you to a place to sit and I'll be a proper hostess. Milk? Sugar?"

"Just black."

She left me in an area with a couch and a pair of chairs grouped around a high-pile rug with an abstract design. A couple of eight-foot-tall bookcases reached a little more than halfway to the ceiling and helped screen the space from the rest of the loft. I walked over to the

window and looked down at Lispenard Street but there
wasn't a whole lot to see.

There was one piece of sculpture in the room and I
was standing in front of it when she came back with the
coffee. It was the head of a woman. Her hair was a nest of
snakes, her face a high–cheekboned, broad–browed mask
of unutterable disappointment.

"That's my Medusa," she said. "Don't meet her eyes.
Her gaze turns men to stone."

"She's very good."

"Thank you."

"She looks so disappointed."

"That's the quality," she agreed. "I didn't know that
until I'd finished her, and then I saw it for myself. You've
got a pretty good eye."

"For disappointment, anyway."

She was an attractive woman. Medium height, a little
more well-fleshed than was strictly fashionable. She wore
faded Levi's and a slate-blue chamois shirt with the
sleeves rolled to the elbows. Her face was heart-shaped,
its contours accentuated by a sharply defined widow's
peak. Her hair, dark brown salted with gray, hung almost to her shoulders. Her gray eyes were large and
well-spaced, and a touch of mascara around them was
the only makeup she wore.

We sat in a pair of chairs at right angles to one another and set our coffee mugs on a table made from a section of tree trunk and a slab of slate. She asked if I'd had
trouble finding her address and I said I hadn't. Then she
said, "Well, shall we talk about Barb Ettinger? Maybe
you can start by telling me why you're interested in her
after all these years."

She'd missed the media coverage of Louis Pinell's arrest. It was news to her that the Icepick Prowler was in custody, so it was also news that her former employee had been killed by someone else.

"So for the first time you're looking for a killer with a motive," she said. "If you'd looked at the time—"

"It might have been easier. Yes."

"And it might be easier now just to look the other way. I don't remember her father. I must have met him, after the murder if not before, but I don't have any recollection of him. I remember her sister. Have you met her?"

"Not yet."

"I don't know what she's like now, but she struck me as a snotty little bitch. But I didn't know her well, and anyway it was nine years ago. That's what I keep coming back to. Everything was nine years ago."

"How did you meet Barbara Ettinger?"

"We ran into each other in the neighborhood. Shopping at the Grand Union, going to the candy store for a paper. Maybe I mentioned that I was running a day-care center. Maybe she heard it from someone else. Either way, one morning she walked into the Happy Hours and asked if I needed any help."

"And you hired her right away?"

"I told her I couldn't pay her much. The place was just about making expenses. I started it for a dumb reason—there was no convenient day-care center in the neighborhood, and I needed a place to dump my own kids, so I found a partner and we opened the Happy

Hours, and instead of dumping my kids I was watching them and everybody else's, and of course my partner came to her senses about the time the ink was dry on the lease, and she backed out and I was running the whole show myself. I told Barb I needed her but I couldn't afford her, and she said she mostly wanted something to do and she'd work cheap. I forget what I paid her but it wasn't a whole lot."

"Was she good at her work?"

"It was essentially baby-sitting. There's a limit to how good you can be at it." She thought for a moment. "It's hard to remember. Nine years ago, so I was twenty-nine at the time, and she was a few years younger."

"She was twenty-six when she died."

"Jesus, that's not very old, is it?" She closed her eyes, wincing at early death. "She was a big help to me, and I guess she was good enough at what she did. She seemed to enjoy it most of the time. She'd have enjoyed it more if she'd been a more contented woman generally."

"She was discontented?"

"I don't know if that's the right word." She turned to glance at her bust of Medusa. "Disappointed? You got the feeling that Barb's life wasn't quite what she'd had in mind for herself. Everything was okay, her husband was okay, her apartment was okay, but she'd hoped for something more than just okay, and she didn't have it."

"Someone described her as restless."

"Restless." She tasted the word. "That fits her well enough. Of course that was a time for women to be restless. Sexual roles were pretty confused and confusing."

"Aren't they still?"

"Maybe they always will be. But I think things are a little more settled now than they were for a while there. She was restless, though. Definitely restless."

"Her marriage was a disappointment?"

"Most of them are, aren't they? I don't suppose it would have lasted, but we'll never know, will we? Is he still with the Welfare Department?"

I brought her up to date on Douglas Ettinger.

"I didn't know him too well," she said. "Barb seemed to feel he wasn't good enough for her. At least I got that impression. His background was low-rent compared to hers. Not that she grew up with the Vanderbilts, but I gather she had a proper suburban childhood and a fancy education. He worked long hours and he had a dead-end job. And yes, there was one other thing wrong with him."

"What was that?"

"He fucked around."

"Did he really or did she just think so?"

"He made a pass at me. Oh, it was no big deal, just a casual, offhand sort of proposition. I was not greatly interested. The man looked like a chipmunk. I wasn't much flattered, either, because one sensed he did this sort of thing a lot and that it didn't mean I was irresistible. Of course I didn't say anything to Barb, but she had evidence of her own. She caught him once at a party, necking in the kitchen with the hostess. And I gather he was dipping into his welfare clients."

"What about his wife?"

"I gather he was dipping into her, too. I don't—"

"Was she having an affair with anybody?"

She leaned forward, took hold of her coffee mug. Her hands were large for a woman, her nails clipped short. I suppose long nails would be an impossible hindrance for a sculptor.

She said, "I was paying her a very low salary. You could almost call it a token salary. I mean, high school kids got a better hourly rate for baby-sitting, and Barb didn't even get to raid the refrigerator. So if she wanted time off, all she did was take it."

"Did she take a lot of time off?"

"Not all that much, but I had the impression that she was taking an occasional afternoon or part of an afternoon for something more exciting than a visit to the dentist. A woman has a different air about her when she's off to meet a lover."

"Did she have that air the day she was killed?"

"I wish you'd asked me nine years ago. I'd have had a better chance of remembering. I know she left early that day but I don't have any memory of the details. You think she met a lover and he killed her?"

"I don't think anything special at this stage. Her husband said she was nervous about the Icepick Prowler."

"I don't think. . .wait a minute. I remember thinking about that afterward, after she'd been killed. That she'd been talking about the danger of living in the city. I don't know if she said anything specific about the Icepick killings, but there was something about feeling as though she was being watched or followed. I interpreted it as a kind of premonition of her own death."

"Maybe it was."

"Or maybe she was being watched and followed. What is it they say? 'Paranoiacs have enemies, too.' Maybe she really sensed something."

"Would she let a stranger into the apartment?"

"I wondered about that at the time. If she was on guard to begin with—"

She broke off suddenly. I asked her what was the matter.

"Nothing."

"I'm a stranger and you let me into your apartment."

"It's a loft. As if it makes a difference. I—"

I took out my wallet and tossed it onto the table between us. "Look through it," I said. "There's an ID in it. It'll match the name I gave you over the phone, and I think there's something with a photograph on it."

"That's not necessary."

, "Look it over anyway. You're not going to be very useful as a subject of interrogation if you're anxious about getting killed. The ID won't prove I'm not a rapist or a murderer, but rapists and murderers don't usually give you their right names ahead of time. Go ahead, pick it up."

She went through the wallet quickly, then handed it back to me. I returned it to my pocket. "That 's a lousy picture of you," she said. "But I guess it's you, all right. I don't think she'd let a stranger into her apartment. She'd let a lover in, though. Or a husband."

"You think her husband killed her?"

"Married people always kill one another. Sometimes it takes them fifty years."

"Any idea who her lover may have been?"

"It may not have been just one person. I'm just guessing, but she could have had an itch to experiment. And she was pregnant so it was safe."

She laughed. I asked her what was so funny.

"I was trying to think where she would have met someone. A neighbor, maybe, or a male half of some couple she and her husband saw socially. It's not as though she could have met men on the job. We had plenty of males there, but unfortunately none of them were over eight years old."

"Not very promising."

"Except that's not altogether true. Sometimes fathers would bring the kids in, or pick them up after work. There are situations more conducive to flirtation, but I had daddies come on to me while they collected their children, and it probably happened to Barbara. She was very attractive, you know. And she didn't wrap herself up in an old Mother Hubbard when she came to work at the Happy Hours. She had a good figure and she dressed to show it off."

The conversation went on a little longer before I got a handle on the question. Then I said, "Did you and Barbara ever become lovers?"

I was watching her eyes when I asked the question, and they widened in response. "Jesus Christ," she said.

I waited her out.

"I'm just wondering where the question came from," she said. "Did somebody say we were lovers? Or am I an obvious dyke or something?"

"I was told you left your husband for another woman."

"Well, that's close. I left my husband for thirty or forty reasons, I suppose. And the first relationship I had after I left him *was* with a woman. Who told you? Not Doug Ettinger. He'd moved out of the neighborhood before that particular shit hit the fan. Unless he happened to talk to somebody. Maybe he and Eddie got together and cried on each other's shoulder about how women are no good, they either get stabbed or they run off with each other. Was it Doug?"

"No. It was a woman who lived in your building on Wyckoff Street."

"Someone in the building. Oh, it must have been Maisie! Except that's not her name. Give me a minute. Mitzi! It was Mitzi Pomerance, wasn't it?"

"I didn't get her first name. I just spoke with her on the telephone."

"Little Mitzi Pomerance. Are they still married? Of course, they'd have to be. Unless he left, but nothing would propel her away from hearth and home. She'd insist her marriage was heaven even if it meant systematically denying every negative emotion that ever threatened to come to the surface. The worst thing about going back to visit the kids was the look on that twit's face when we passed on the stairs." She sighed and shook her head at the memory. "I never had anything going with Barbara. Strangely enough, I never had anything going with anybody, male or female, before I split with Eddie. And the woman I got together with afterward was the first woman I ever slept with in my life."

"But you were attracted to Barbara Ettinger."

"Was I? I recognized that she was attractive. That's not the same thing. Was I specifically attracted to her?" She weighed the notion. "Maybe," she conceded. "Not on any conscious level, I don't think. And when I did begin to consider the possibility that I might find it, oh, interesting to go to bed with a woman, I don't think I had any particular woman in mind. As a matter of fact, I don't even think I entertained the fantasy while Barbara was alive."

"I have to ask these personal questions."

"You don't have to apologize. Jesus, Mitzi Pomerance. I'll bet she's fat, I'll bet she's a plump little piglet by now. But you only spoke to her over the phone."

"That's right."

"Is she still living in the same place? She must be. You wouldn't get them out of there with a crowbar."

"Somebody did. A buyer converted the house to one-family."

"They must have been sick. Did they stay in the neighborhood?"

"More or less. They moved to Carroll Street."

"Well, I hope they're happy. Mitzi and Gordon." She leaned forward, searched my face with her gray eyes. "You drink," she said. "Right?"

"Pardon?"

"You're a drunk, aren't you?"

"I suppose you could call me a drinking man."

The words sounded stiff, even to me. They hung in the air for a moment and then her laughter cut in, full-bodied and rich. "'I suppose you could call me a drinking man.' Jesus, that's wonderful. Well, I suppose you could call me a drinking woman, Mr. Scudder. People have called me a good deal worse, and it's been a long day and a dry one. How about a little something to cut the dust?"

"That's not a bad idea."

"What'll it be?"

"Do you have bourbon?"

"I don't think so." The bar was behind a pair of sliding doors in one of the bookcases. "Scotch or vodka," she announced.

"Scotch."

"Rocks? Water? What?"

"Just straight."

"The way God made it, huh?" She brought back a pair of rocks glasses filled about halfway, one with Scotch, the other with vodka. She gave me mine, looked into her own. She had the air of someone trying to select a toast, but evidently she couldn't think of one. "Oh, what the hell," she said, and took a drink.

Who do you think killed her?"

"Too early to tell. It could have been somebody I haven't heard of yet. Or it could have been Pinell. I'd like ten minutes with him."

"You think you could refresh his memory?"

I shook my head. "I think I might get some sense of him. So much detection is intuition. You gather details and soak up impressions, and then the answer pops into your mind out of nowhere. It's not like Sherlock Holmes, at least it never was for me."

"You make it sound almost as though there's a psychic element to the process."

"Well, I can't read palms or see the future. But maybe there is." I sipped Scotch. It had that medicinal taste that Scotch has but I didn't mind it as much as I usually do. It was one of the heavier Scotches, dark and peaty. Teacher's, I think it was. "I want to get out to Sheepshead Bay next," I said.

"Now?"

"Tomorrow. That's where the fourth Icepick killing took place, and that was the one that's supposed to have spooked Barbara Ettinger."

"You think the same person—"

"Louis Pinell admits to the Sheepshead Bay murder. Of course that doesn't prove anything, either. I'm not sure why I want to go out there. I guess I want to talk to somebody who was on the scene, someone who saw the body. There were some physical details about the killings that were held back from the press coverage, and they were duplicated in Barbara's murder. Imperfectly duplicated, and I want to know if there was any parallel in the other Brooklyn homicide."

"And if there was, what would it prove? That there was a second killer, a maniac who confined himself to Brooklyn?"

"And who conveniently stopped at two killings? It's possible. It wouldn't even rule out someone with a motive for killing Barbara. Say her husband decided to kill her, but he realized the Icepick Prowler hadn't been to Brooklyn yet, so he killed some stranger in Sheepshead Bay first to establish a pattern."

"Do people do things like that?"

"There's nothing you can imagine that somebody hasn't done at one time or another. Maybe somebody had a motive for killing the woman in Sheepshead Bay. Then he was worried that the murder would stand out as the only one of its kind in Brooklyn, so he went after Barbara. Or maybe that was just his excuse. Maybe he killed a second time because he'd found out that he enjoyed it."

"God." She drank vodka. "What was the physical detail?"

"You don't want to know about it."

"You protecting the little woman from the awful truth?"

"The victims were stabbed through the eyes. An icepick, right through the eyeballs."

"Jesus. And the. . .what did you call it? Imperfect duplication?"

"Barbara Ettinger just got it in one eye."

"Like a wink." She sat for a long moment, then looked down at her glass and noticed that it was empty. She went to the bar and came back with both bottles. After she'd filled our glasses she left the bottles on the slate-topped table.

"I wonder why he would do a thing like that," she said.

"That's another reason I'd like to see Pinell," I said. "To ask him."

The conversation turned this way and that. At one point she asked whether she should call me Matt or Matthew. I told her it didn't matter to me. She said it mattered to her that I call her not Janice but Jan.

"Unless you're uncomfortable calling murder suspects by their first names."

When I was a cop I learned always to call suspects by their first names. It gave you a certain amount of psychological leverage. I told her she wasn't a suspect.

"I was at the Happy Hours all that afternoon," she said. "Of course it would be hard to prove after all these years. At the time it would have been easy. Alibis must be harder to come by for people who live alone."

"You live alone here?"

"Unless you count the cats. They're hiding somewhere. They steer clear of strangers. Showing them your ID wouldn't impress them much."

"Real hard-liners."

"Uh-huh. I've always lived alone. Since I left Eddie, that is. I've been in relationships but I always lived alone."

"Unless we count the cats."

"Unless we count the cats. I never thought at the time that I'd be living by myself for the next eight years. I thought a relationship with a woman might be different in some fundamental way. See, back then was consciousness-raising time. I decided the problem was men."

"And it wasn't?"

"Well, it may have been one of the problems. Women turned out to be another problem. For a while I decided I was one of those fortunate people who are capable of relationships with both sexes."

"Just for a while?"

"Uh-huh. Because what I discovered next was that I may be capable of relationships with men and women, but what I mostly am is not very good at relationships."

"Well, I can relate to that."

"I figured you probably could. You live alone, don't you, Matthew?"

"For a while now."

"Your sons are with your wife? I'm not psychic. There's a picture of them in your wallet."

"Oh, that. It's an old picture."

"They're handsome boys."

"They're good kids, too." I added a little Scotch to my glass. "They live out in Syosset. They'll take the train in now and then and we catch a ball game together, or maybe a fight in the Garden."

"They must enjoy that."

"I know I enjoy it."

"You must have moved out a while ago."

I nodded. "Around the time I left the cops."

"Same reason?"

I shrugged.

"How come you quit the cops? Was it this stuff?"

"What stuff?"

She waved a hand at the bottles. "You know. The booze."

"Oh, hell, no," I said. "I wasn't even that heavy a hitter at the time. I just reached a point where I didn't feel like being a cop anymore."

"What did it? Disillusionment? A lack of faith in the criminal justice system? Disgust with corruption?"

I shook my head. "I lost my illusions early in the game and I never had much faith in the criminal justice system. It's a terrible system and the cops just do what they can. As far as corruption goes, I was never enough of an idealist to be bothered by it."

"What then? Mid-life crisis?"

"You could call it that."

"Well, we won't talk about it if you don't want to."

We fell silent for a moment. She drank and then I drank, and then I put my glass down and said, "Well, it's no secret. It's just not something I talk about a lot. I was in a tavern up in Washington Heights one night. It was a place where cops could drink on the arm. The owner liked having us around so you could run a tab and never be asked for payment. I had every right to be there. I was off-duty and I wanted to unwind a little before I drove back out to the island."

Or maybe I wouldn't have gone home that night anyway. I didn't always. Sometimes I caught a few hours' sleep in a hotel room to save driving back and forth. Sometimes I didn't have to get a hotel room.

"Two punks held up the place," I went on. "They got what was in the register and shot the bartender on the way out, shot him dead just for the hell of it. I ran out

into the street after them. I was in plainclothes but of
course I was carrying a gun. You always carry it.

"I emptied the gun at them. I got them both. I killed
one of them and crippled the other. Left him paralyzed
from the waist down. Two things he'll never do again are
walk and fuck."

I'd told this story before but this time I could feel it all
happening again. Washington Heights is hilly and they'd
taken off up an incline. I remembered bracing myself,
holding the gun with both hands, firing uphill at them.
Maybe it was the Scotch that was making the recollection
so vivid. Maybe it was something I responded to in her
big unwavering gray eyes.

"And because you killed one and crippled another—"

I shook my head. "That wouldn't have bothered me.
I'm only sorry I didn't kill them both. They murdered
that bartender for no good reason on God's earth. I
wouldn't lose a dime's worth of sleep over those two."

She waited.

"One of the shots went wide," I said. "Shooting uphill
at a pair of moving targets, hell, it's remarkable I scored
as well as I did. I always shot Expert on the police range,
but it's different when it's real." I tried to draw my eyes
away from hers but couldn't manage it. "One shot
missed, though, and it ricocheted off the pavement or
something. Took a bad hop. And there was a little girl
walking around or standing around, whatever the hell
she was doing. She was only six years old. I don't know
what the hell she was doing out at that hour."

This time I looked away. "The bullet went into her
eye," I said. "The ricochet took off some of its steam so if
it had been an inch to the side one way or the other it
probably would have glanced off bone, but life's a game

of inches, isn't it? There was no bone to get in the way and the bullet wound up in her brain and she died. Instantly."

"God."

"I didn't do anything wrong. There was a departmental investigation because that's standard procedure, and it was agreed unanimously that I hadn't done anything wrong. As a matter of fact I received a commendation. The child was Hispanic, Puerto Rican, Estrellita Rivera her name was, and sometimes the press gets on you when there's a minority group casualty like that, or you get static from community groups, but there was none of that in this case. If I was anything I was a fast-acting hero cop who had a piece of bad luck."

"And you quit the police force."

The Scotch bottle was empty. There was maybe half a pint of vodka in the other bottle and I poured a few ounces of it into my glass. "Not right away," I said, "but before too long. And I don't know what made me do it."

"Guilt."

"I'm not sure. All I know is that being a cop didn't seem to be fun anymore. Being a husband and a father didn't seem to work, either. I took a leave of absence from both, moved into a hotel a block west of Columbus Circle. Somewhere down the line it became clear that I wasn't going back, not to my wife, not to the department."

Neither of us said anything for a while. After a moment she leaned over and touched my hand. It was an unexpected and slightly awkward gesture and for some reason it touched me. I felt a thickening in my throat.

Then she had withdrawn her hand and was on her feet. I thought for a moment that she meant for me to leave. Instead she said, "I'm going to call the liquor store while they're still open. The nearest place is on Canal and they close early. Do you want to stick with Scotch or would you rather switch to bourbon? And what brand of bourbon?"

"I should probably be going soon."

"Scotch or bourbon?"

"I'll stay with the Scotch."

While we waited for the liquor delivery she took me around the loft and showed me some of her work. Most of it was realistic, like the Medusa, but a few pieces were abstract. There was a lot of strength in her sculpture. I told her I liked her work.

"I'm pretty good," she said.

She wouldn't let me pay for the liquor, insisting that I was her guest. We sat in our chairs again, opened our respective bottles, filled our glasses. She asked me if I really liked her work. I assured her that I did.

"I'm supposed to be good," she said. "You know how I got into this? Playing with clay with the kids at the day-care center. I wound up taking the clay home, that yellow modeling clay, and working with it by the hour. Then I took a night course at Brooklyn College, an Adult Ed class, and the instructor told me I had talent. He didn't have to tell me. I knew it.

"I've had some recognition. I had a show at the Chuck Levitan Gallery a little over a year ago. You know the gallery? On Grand Street?" I didn't. "Well, he gave me a one-man show. A one-woman show. A one-person show. Shit, you have to think before you talk nowadays, have you noticed?"

"Uh-huh."

"And I had an NEA grant last year. National Endowment for the Arts. Plus a smaller grant from the Einhoorn Foundation. Don't pretend you heard of the Einhoorn Foundation. I never heard of it before I got the grant. I've got pieces in some fairly decent collections. One or two in museums. Well, one, and it's not MOMA, but it's a museum. I'm a sculptor."

"I never said you weren't."

"And my kids are in California and I never see them. He has full custody. The hell, I moved out, right? I'm some kind of unnatural woman in the first place, some dyke who deserts husband and kids, so of course he gets custody, right? I didn't make an issue of it. Do you want to know something, Matthew?"

"What?"

"I didn't *want* custody. I was done with day care. I had fucking had it with kids, my own included. What do you make of that?"

"It sounds natural enough."

"The Maisie Pomperances of the world wouldn't agree with you. Excuse me, I mean Mitzi. Gordon and Mitzi Fucking Pomerance. Mr. and Mrs. High School Yearbook."

I was able to hear the vodka in her voice now. She wasn't slurring her words any but there was a timbre to her speech that the alcohol had provided. It didn't surprise me. She had matched me drink for drink and I was hitting it pretty good myself. Of course I'd had a head start on her.

"When he said he was moving to California I threw a fit. Yelled that it wasn't fair, that he had to stay in New York so I could visit them. I had visitation rights, I said, and what good were my visitation rights if they were three thousand miles away? But do you know something?"

"What?"

"I was relieved. Part of me was glad they were going, because you wouldn't believe what it was like, traipsing out there on the subway once a week, sitting in the apartment with them or walking around Boerum Hill and always risking blank stares from Maisie Pomerance. Goddamn it, why can't I even get that goddamned woman's name right? Mitzi!"

"I've got her number written down. You could always call her up and tell her off."

She laughed. "Oh, Jesus," she said. "I gotta pee. I'll be right back."

When she came back she sat on the couch. Without preamble she said, "You know what we are? Me with my sculpture and you with your existential angst, and what we are is a couple of drunks who copped out. That's all."

"If you say so."

"Don't patronize me. Let's face it. We're both alcoholics."

"I'm a heavy drinker. That's a difference."

"What's the difference?"

"I could stop anytime I want to."

"Then why don't you?"

"Why should I?"

Instead of answering the question she leaned forward to fill her glass. "I stopped for a while," she said. "I quit cold for two months. More than two months."

"You just up and quit?"

"I went to AA."

"Oh."

"You ever been?"

I shook my head. "I don't think it would work for me."

"But you could stop anytime you want."

"Yeah, if *I* wanted."

"And anyway you're not an alcoholic."

I didn't say anything at first. Then I said, "I suppose it depends on how you define the word. Anyway, all it is is a label."

"They say you decide for yourself if you're an alcoholic."

"Well, I'm deciding that I'm not."

"I decided I was. And it worked for me. The thing is, they say it works best if you don't drink."

"I can see where that might make a difference."

"I don't know why I got on this subject." She drained her glass, looked at me over its rim. "I didn't mean to get on this goddamned subject. First my kids and then my drinking, what a fucking down."

"It's all right."

"I'm sorry, Matthew."

"Forget it."

"Sit next to me and help me forget it."

I joined her on the couch and ran a hand over her fine hair. The sprinkling of gray enhanced its attractiveness. She looked at me for a moment out of those bottomless gray eyes, then let the lids drop. I kissed her and she clung to me.

We necked some. I touched her breasts, kissed her throat. Her strong hands worked the muscles in my back and shoulders like modeling clay.

"You'll stay over," she said.

"I'd like that."

"So would I."

I freshened both our drinks.

NINE

I awakened with church bells pealing in the distance. My head was clear and I felt good. I swung my legs over the side of the bed and met the eyes of a long-haired cat curled up at the foot of the bed on the other side. He looked me over, then tucked his head in and resumed napping. Sleep with the lady of the house and the cats accept you.

I got dressed and found Jan in the kitchen. She was drinking a glass of pale orange juice. I figured there was something in it to take the edge off her hangover. She'd made coffee in a Chemex filter pot and poured me a cup. I stood by the window and drank it.

We didn't talk. The church bells had taken a break and the Sunday morning silence stretched out. It was a bright day out, the sun burning away in a cloudless sky. I looked down and couldn't see a single sign of life, not a person on the street, not a car moving.

I finished my coffee and added the cup to the dirty dishes in the stainless-steel sink. Jan used a key to bring the elevator to the floor. She asked if I was going out to Sheepshead Bay and I said I guessed I was. We held onto each other for a moment. I felt the warmth of her fine body through the robe she was wearing.

"I'll call you," I said, and rode the oversized elevator to the ground.

An Officer O'Byrne gave me directions over the phone. I followed them, riding the BMT Brighton Line to Gravesend Neck Road. The train came up above ground level at some point after it crossed into Brooklyn, and we rode through some neighborhoods of detached houses with yards that didn't look like New York at all.

The station house for the Sixty-first Precinct was on Coney Island Avenue and I managed to find it without too much trouble. In the squad room I played do-you-know with a wiry, long-jawed detective named Antonelli. We knew enough of the same people for him to relax with me. I told him what I was working on and mentioned that Frank Fitzroy had steered it my way. He knew Frank, too, though I didn't get the impression that they were crazy about each other.

"I'll see what our file looks like," he said. "But you probably saw copies of our reports in the file Fitzroy showed you."

"What I mostly want is to talk with somebody who looked at the body."

"Wouldn't the names of officers on the scene be in the file you saw in Manhattan?"

I'd thought of that myself. Maybe I could have managed all this without coming out to the ass end of Brooklyn. But when you go out and look for something you occasionally find more than you knew you were looking for.

"Well, maybe I can find that file," he said, and left me at an old wooden desk scarred with cigarette burns along its edges. Two desks over, a black detective with his sleeves rolled up was talking on the phone. It sounded as though he was talking to a woman, and it didn't sound much like police business. At another desk along the far wall a pair of cops, one uniformed and one in a suit, were questioning a teenager with a mop of unruly yellow hair. I couldn't hear what they were saying.

Antonelli came back with a slim file and dropped it on the desk in front of me. I went through it, pausing now and then to make a note in my notebook. The victim, I learned, was a Susan Potowski of 2705 Haring Street. She'd been a mother of two, twenty-nine years old, separated from her husband, a construction laborer. She lived with her kids in the lower flat of a two-family semi-detached house, and she'd been killed around two o'clock on a Wednesday afternoon.

Her kids found her. They came home from school together around three thirty, a boy of eight and a girl of ten, and they found their mother on the kitchen floor, her clothing partly removed, her body covered with stab wounds. They ran around the street screaming until the beat cop turned up.

"Finding anything?"

"Maybe," I said. I copied down the names of the first cop on the scene, added those of two detectives from the Six-One who'd gone to the Haring Street house before switching the case to Midtown North. I showed the three names to Antonelli. "Any of these guys still work out of here?"

"Patrolman Burton Havermeyer, Detective Third-Grade Kenneth Allgood, Detective First-Grade Michael Quinn. Mick Quinn died two, maybe three years ago. Line of duty. He and a partner had a liquor store staked out on Avenue W and there were shots exchanged and he was killed. Terrible thing. Lost a wife to cancer two years before that, so he left four kids all alone in the world, the oldest just starting college. You must have read about it."

"I think I did."

"Guys who shot him pulled good long time. But they're alive and he's dead, so go figure. The other two, Allgood and Havermeyer, I don't even know the names, so they've been off the Six-One since before my time, which is what? Five years? Something like that."

"Can you find out where they went?"

"I can probably find out something. What do you want to ask 'em, anyway?"

"If she was stabbed in both eyes."

"Wasn't there an ME's report in the file whats-his-name showed you? Fitzroy?"

I nodded. "Both eyes."

"So?"

"Remember that case some years ago? They pulled some woman out of the Hudson, called it death by drowning? Then some genius in the Medical Examiner's office took the skull and started using it for a paper-weight, and there was a scandal about that, and because of all the heat somebody finally took a good look at the skull for the first time and found a bullet hole in it."

"I remember. She was some woman from New Jersey, married to a doctor, wasn't she?"

"That's right."

"I got a rule-of-thumb. When a doctor's wife gets killed, he did it. I don't give a shit about the evidence. The doc always did it. I don't remember whether this one got off or not."

"Neither do I."

"I take your point, though. The ME's report isn't something you want to run to the bank with. But how good is a witness to something that happened nine years ago?"

"Not too good. Still—"

"I'll see what I can see."

He was gone a little longer this time, and he had a funny expression on his face when he returned. "Bad luck case," he said. "Allgood's dead, too. And the patrolman, Havermeyer, he left the department."

"How did Allgood die?"

"Heart attack, about a year ago. He got transferred out a couple of years back. He was working out of Centre Street headquarters. Collapsed at his desk one day and died. One of the guys in the file room knew him from when he worked here and happened to know how he died. Havermeyer could be dead, too, for all I know."

"What happened to him?"

He shrugged. "Who knows? He put in his papers just a few months after the Icepick thing. Cited unspecified personal reasons for returning to civilian life. He'd only been in for two, three years. You know what the drop-out rate's like for the new ones. Hell, you're a drop-out yourself. Personal reasons, right?"

"Something like that."

"I dug up an address and a number. He probably moved six times between then and now. If he didn't leave a trail, you can always try downtown. He wasn't here long enough to have any pension rights but they usually keep track of ex-cops."

"Maybe he's still in the same place."

"Could be. My grandmother's still living in three little rooms on Elizabeth Street, same apartment she's been in since she got off the boat from Palermo. Some people stay put. Other change their houses like they change their socks. Maybe you'll get lucky. Anything else I can do for you?"

"Where's Haring Street?"

"The murder scene?" He laughed. "Jesus, you're a bloodhound," he said. "Want to get the scent, huh?"

He told me how to walk there. He'd given me a fair amount of his time but he didn't want any money for it. I sensed that he probably didn't—some do and some don't—but I made the offer. "You could probably use a new hat," I said, and he came back with a tight grin and assured me that he had a whole closetful of hats. "And I hardly ever wear a hat these days," he said. I'd been offering him twenty-five dollars, cheap enough for the effort he'd expended. "It's a slow day at a quiet precinct," he said, "and how much mileage can you get out of what I just gave you? You got anybody in mind for that Boerum Hill killing?"

"Not really."

"Like hunting a black cat in a coal mine," he said. "Do me one favor? Let me know how it comes out. *If* it comes out."

I followed his directions to Haring Street. I don't suppose the neighborhood had changed much in nine years.

The houses were well kept up and there were kids all over the place. There were cars parked at the curb, cars in most of the driveways. It occurred to me that there were probably a dozen people on the block who remembered Susan Potowski, and for all I knew her estranged husband had moved back into the house after the murder and lived there now with his children. They'd be older now, seventeen and nineteen.

She must have been young when she had the first one. Nineteen herself. Early marriage and early childbirth wouldn't have been uncommon in that neighborhood.

He probably moved away, I decided. Assuming he came back for the kids, he wouldn't make them go on living in the house where they found their mother dead on the kitchen floor. Would he?

I didn't ring that doorbell, or any other doorbells. I wasn't investigating Susan Potowski's murder and I didn't have to sift her ashes. I took a last look at the house she'd died in, then turned and walked away.

The address I had for Burton Havermeyer was 212 St. Marks Place. The East Village wasn't that likely a place for a cop to live, and it didn't seem terribly likely that he'd still be there nine years later, on or off the force. I called the number Antonelli had given me from a drugstore phone booth on Ocean Avenue.

A woman answered. I asked if I could speak to Mr. Havermeyer. There was a pause. "Mr. Havermeyer doesn't live here."

I started to apologize for having the wrong number but she wasn't through. "I don't know where Mr. Havermeyer can be reached," she said.

"Is this Mrs. Havermeyer?"

"Yes."

I said, "I'm sorry to disturb you, Mrs. Havermeyer. A detective at the Sixty-first Precinct where your husband used to work supplied this number. I'm trying to—"

"My former husband."

There was a toneless quality to her speech, as if she was deliberately detaching herself from the words she was speaking. I had noted a similar characteristic in the speech of recovered mental patients.

"I'm trying to reach him in connection with a police matter," I said.

"He hasn't been a policeman in years."

"I realize that. Do you happen to know how I can get hold of him?"

"No."

"I gather you don't see him often, Mrs. Havermeyer, but would you have any idea—"

"I never see him."

"I see."

"Oh, do you? I never see my former husband. I get a check once a month. It's sent directly to my bank and deposited to my account. I don't see my husband and I don't see the check. Do you see? Do you?"

The words might have been delivered with passion. But the voice remained flat and uninvolved.

I didn't say anything.

"He's in Manhattan," she said. "Perhaps he has a phone, and perhaps it's in the book. You could look it up.

I know you'll excuse me if I don't offer to look it up for you."

"Certainly."

"I'm sure it's important," she said. "Police business always is, isn't it?"

There was no Manhattan telephone book at the drugstore so I let the Information operator look for me. She found a Burton Havermeyer on West 103rd Street. I dialed the number and no one answered.

The drugstore had a lunch counter. I sat on a stool and ate a grilled cheese sandwich and a too-sweet piece of cherry pie and drank two cups of black coffee. The coffee wasn't bad, but it couldn't compare with the stuff Jan had brewed in her Chemex filter pot.

I thought about her. Then I went to the phone again and almost dialed her number, but tried Havermeyer again instead. This time he answered.

I said, "Burton Havermeyer? My name's Matthew Scudder. I wondered if I could come around and see you this afternoon."

"What about?"

"It's a police matter. Some questions I'd like to ask you. I won't take up much of your time."

"You're a police officer?"

Hell. "I used to be one."

"So did I. Could you tell me what you want with me, Mr....?"

"Scudder," I supplied. "It's ancient history, actually. I'm a detective now and I'm working on a case you were involved with when you were with the Six-One."

"That was years ago."

"I know."

"Can't we do this over the phone? I can't imagine what information I could possibly have that would be useful to you. I was a beat patrolman, I didn't work on cases. I—"

"I'd like to drop by if it's all right."

"Well, I—"

"I won't take up much of your time."

There was a pause. "It's my day off," he said, in what was not quite a whine. "I just figured to sit around, have a couple of beers, watch a ball game."

"We can talk during the commercials."

He laughed. "Okay, you win. You know the address? The name's on the bell. When should I expect you?"

"An hour, hour and a half."

"Good enough."

The Upper West Side is another neighborhood on the upswing, but the local renaissance hasn't crossed Ninety-sixth Street yet. Havermeyer lived on 103rd between Columbus and Amsterdam in one of the rundown brownstones that lined both sides of the street. The neighborhood was mostly Spanish. There were a lot of people sitting on the stoops, listening to enormous portable radios and drinking Miller High Life out of brown paper bags. Every third woman was pregnant.

I found the right building and rang the right bell and climbed four flights of stairs. He was waiting for me in the doorway of one of the back apartments. He said, "Scudder?" and I nodded. "Burt Havermeyer," he said. "Come on in."

I followed him into a fair-sized studio with a Pullman kitchen. The overhead light fixture was a bare bulb in one of those Japanese paper shades. The walls were due for paint. I took a seat on the couch and accepted the can of beer he handed me. He popped one for himself, then moved to turn off the television set, a black and white portable perched on top of an orange crate that held paperback books on its lower two shelves.

He pulled up a chair for himself, crossed his legs. He looked to be in his early thirties, five-eight or -nine, pale complected, with narrow shoulders and a beer gut. He wore brown gabardine slacks and a brown and beige patterned sportshirt. He had deep-set brown eyes, heavy jowls and slicked-down dark brown hair, and he hadn't shaved that morning. Neither, come to think of it, had I.

"About nine years ago," I said. "A woman named Susan Potowski."

"I knew it."

"Oh."

"I hung up and thought, why's anybody want to talk with me about some case nine or ten years old? Then I figured it had to be the icepick thing. I read the papers. They got the guy, right? They made a lap and he fell in it."

"That's about it." I explained how Louis Pinell had denied a role in the death of Barbara Ettinger and how the facts appeared to bear him out.

"I don't get it," he said. "That still leaves something like eight killings, doesn't it? Isn't that enough to put him away?"

"It's not enough for the Ettinger woman's father. He wants to know who killed his daughter."

"And that's your job." He whistled softly. "Lucky you."

"That's about it." I drank a little beer from the can. "I don't suppose there's any connection between the Potowski killing and the one I'm investigating, but they're both in Brooklyn and maybe Pinell didn't do either of them. You were the first police officer on the scene. You remember that day pretty well?"

"Jesus," he said. "I ought to."

"Oh?"

"I left the force because of it. But I suppose they told you that out in Sheepshead Bay."

"All they said was unspecified personal reasons."

"That right?" He held his beer can in both hands and sat with his head bowed, looking down at it. "I remember how her kids screamed," he said. "I remember knowing I was going to walk in on something really bad, and then the next memory I have is I'm in her kitchen looking down at the body. One of the kids is hanging onto my pants leg the way kids do, you know how they do, and I'm looking down at her and I close my eyes and open 'em again and the picture doesn't change. She was in a whatchacallit, a housecoat. It had like Japanese writing on it and a picture of a bird, Japanese-style art. A kimono? I guess you call it a kimono. I remember the color. Orange, with black trim.

He looked up at me, then dropped his eyes again. "The housecoat was open. The kimono. Partially open. There were these dots all over her body, like punctuation marks. Where he got her with the icepick. Mostly the torso. She had very nice breasts. That's a terrible thing to remember but how do you quit remembering? Standing there noticing all the wounds in her breasts, and she's dead. And still noticing that she's got a first-rate pair of tits. And hating yourself for thinking it."

"It happens."

"I know, I know, but it sticks in your mind like a bone caught in your throat. And the kids wailing, and noises outside. At first I don't hear any of the noise because the sight of her just blocks everything else. Like it deafens you, knocks out the other senses. Do you know what I mean?"

"Yes."

"Then the sound comes up, and the kid's still hanging on my pants leg, and if he lives to be a hundred that's how he's gonna remember his mother. Myself, I never saw her before in my life, and I couldn't get that picture out of my head. It repeated on me night and day. When I slept it got in my nightmares and during the day it would come into my mind at odd moments. I didn't want to go in anyplace. I didn't want to risk coming up on another dead body. And it dawned on me finally that I didn't want to stay in a line of work where when people get killed it's up to you to deal with it. 'Unspecified personal reasons.' Well, I just specified. I gave it a little time and it didn't wear off and I quit."

"What do you do now?"

"Security guard." He named a midtown store. "I tried a couple of other things but I've had this job for seven years now. I wear a uniform and I even have a gun on my hip. Job I had before this, you wore a gun but it wasn't loaded. That drove me nuts. I said I'd carry a gun or not carry a gun, it didn't matter to me, but don't give me an unloaded gun because then the bad guys think you're armed but you can't defend yourself. Now I got a loaded gun and it hasn't been out of the holster in seven

years and that's the way I like it. I'm a deterrent to rob-
bery and shoplifting. Not as much of a deterrent to shoplifting as we'd like. Boosters can be pretty slick."

"I can imagine."

"It's dull work. I like that. I like knowing I don't have
to walk into somebody's kitchen and there's death on the
floor. I joke with other people on the job, I hook a shop-
lifter now and then, and the whole thing's nice and
steady. I got a simple life, you know what I mean? I like
it that way."

"A question about the murder scene."

"Sure."

"The woman's eyes."

"Oh, Christ," he said. "You had to remind me."

"Tell me."

"Her eyes were open. He stabbed all the victims in the
eyes. I didn't know that. It was kept out of the papers, the
way they'll hold something back, you know? But when
the detectives got there they saw it right away and that
cinched it, you know, that it wasn't our case and we
could buck it on up to some other precinct. I forget which
one."

"Midtown South."

"If you say so." He closed his eyes for a moment.
"Did I say her eyes were open? Staring up at the ceiling.
But they were like ovals of blood."

"Both eyes?"

"Pardon?"

"Were both of her eyes the same?"

He nodded. "Why?"

"Barbara Ettinger was only stabbed in one eye."

"It make a difference?"

"I don't know."

"If somebody was going to copy the killer, they'd copy him completely, wouldn't they?"

"You'd think so."

"Unless it *was* him and he was rushed for a change. Who knows with a crazy person, anyway? Maybe this time God told him only stab one eye. Who knows?"

He went for another beer and offered me one but I passed. I didn't want to hang around long enough to drink it. I had really only had one question to ask him and his answer had done nothing but confirm the medical report. I suppose I could have asked it over the phone, but then I wouldn't have had the same chance to probe his memory and get a real sense of what he'd found in that kitchen. No question now that he'd gone back in time and seen Susan Potowski's body all over again. He wasn't guessing that she'd been stabbed in both eyes. He had closed his own eyes and seen the wounds.

He said, "Sometimes I wonder. Well, when I read about them arresting this Pinell, and now with you coming over here. Suppose I wasn't the one walked in on the Potowski woman? Or suppose it happened three years later when I had that much more experience? I can see how my whole life might have been different."

"You might have stayed on the force."

"It's possible, right? I don't know if I really liked being a cop or if I was any good at it. I liked the classes at the Academy. I liked wearing the uniform. I liked walking the beat and saying hello to people and having them say hello back. Actual police work, I don't know how much I liked it. Maybe if I was really cut out for it I wouldn't have been thrown for a loop by what I saw in that kitchen. Or I would have toughed it out and gotten over it eventually. You were a cop yourself and you quit, right?"

"For unspecified personal reasons."

"Yeah, I guess there's a lot of that going around."

"There was a death involved," I said. "A child. What happened, I lost my taste for the work."

"Exactly what happened to me, Matt. I lost my taste for it. You know what I think? If it wasn't that one particular thing it would have been something else."

Could I say the same thing? It was not a thought that had occurred to me previously. If Estrellita Rivera had been home in bed where she belonged, would I still be living in Syosset and carrying a badge? Or would some other incident have given me an inevitable nudge in a direction I had to walk?

I said, "You and your wife separated."

"That's right."

"Same time you put in your papers?"

"Not too long after that."

"You move here right away?"

"I was in an SRO hotel a couple blocks down on Broadway. I stayed there for maybe ten weeks until I found this place. Been here ever since."

"Your wife's still in the East Village."

"Huh?"

"St. Marks Place. She's still living there."

"Oh. Right."

"Any kids?"

"No."

"Makes it easier."

"I guess so."

"My wife and sons are out on Long Island. I'm in a hotel on Fifty-seventh Street."

He nodded, understanding. People move and their lives change. He'd wound up guarding cashmere sweaters. I'd wound up doing whatever it is I do. Looking in a coal mine for a black cat, according to Antonelli. Looking for a cat that wasn't even there.

TEN

When I got back to my hotel there was a message from Lynn London. I called her from the pay phone in the lobby and explained who I was and what I wanted.

She said, "My father hired you? It's funny he didn't say anything to me. I thought they had the man who killed my sister. Why would he suddenly—well, let's let it ride for now. I don't know what help I could be."

I said I'd like to meet with her to talk about her sister.

"Not tonight," she said briskly. "I just got back from the mountains a couple of hours ago. I'm exhausted and I've got to do my lesson plans for the week."

"Tomorrow?"

"I teach during the day. I've got a dinner date and I'm going to a concert after that. Tuesday's my group therapy night. Maybe Wednesday? That's not terribly good for me either. Hell."

"Maybe we could—"

"Maybe we could handle it over the phone? I don't really know very much, Mr. Scudder, and God knows I'm beat at the moment, but perhaps I could deal with, say, ten minutes' worth of questions right now, because otherwise I honestly don't know when we could get together. I don't really know very much, it was a great many years ago and—"

"When do you finish your classes tomorrow afternoon?"

"Tomorrow afternoon? We dismiss the children at three fifteen, but—"

"I'll meet you at your apartment at four."

"I told you. I have a dinner date tomorrow."

"And a concert after it. I'll meet you at four. I won't take that much of your time."

She wasn't thrilled, but that's how we left it. I spent another dime and called Jan Keane. I recapped the day and she told me she was in awe of my industriousness. "I don't know," I said. "Sometimes I think I'm just putting in time. I could have accomplished the same thing today with a couple of phone calls."

"We could have handled our business over the phone last night," she said. "As far as that goes."

"I'm glad we didn't."

"So am I," she said. "I think. On the other hand, I was planning on working today and I couldn't even look at clay. I'm just hoping this hangover wears off by bedtime."

"I had a clear head this morning."

"Mine's just beginning to clear now. Maybe my mistake was staying in the house. The sun might have burned off some of the fog. Now I'm just sitting around until it's a reasonable hour to go to sleep."

There might have been an unspoken invitation in that last sentence. I probably could have invited myself over. But I was already home, and a short and quiet evening had its appeal. I told her I'd wanted to say how I'd enjoyed her company and that I'd call her.

"I'm glad you called," she said. "You're a sweet man, Matthew." A pause, and then she said, "I've been thinking about it. He probably did it."

"He?"

"Doug Ettinger. He probably killed her."

"Why?"

"I don't know why. People always have motives to kill their spouses, don't they? There was never a day when I didn't have a reason to kill Eddie."

"I meant why do you think he did it."

"Oh. What I was thinking, I was thinking how devious you would have to be to kill someone and imitate another murder. And I realized what a devious man he was, what a sneak. He could plan something like that."

"That's interesting."

"Listen, I don't have any special knowledge. But it's what I was thinking earlier. And now he's doing what? Selling sporting goods? Is that what you said?"

I sat in my room and read for a while, then had dinner around the corner at Armstrong's. I stayed there for a couple of hours but didn't have very much to drink. The crowd was a light one, as it usually is on a Sunday. I talked to a few people but mostly sat alone and let the events of the past two days thread their way in and out of my consciousness.

I made it an early night, walked down to Eighth Avenue for the early edition of Monday's *News*. Went back to my room, read the paper, took a shower. Looked at myself in the mirror. Thought about shaving, decided to wait until morning.

Had a nightcap, a short one. Went to bed.

I was deep in a dream when the phone rang. I was running in the dream, chasing someone or being chased, and I sat up in bed with my heart pounding.

The phone was ringing. I reached out, answered it.

A woman said, "Why don't you let the dead bury the dead?"

"Who is this?"

"Leave the dead alone. Let the dead stay buried."

"Who is this?"

A click. I turned on a light and looked at my watch. It was around one thirty. I'd been sleeping an hour, if that.

Who had called me? It was a voice I'd heard before but I couldn't place it. Lynn London? I didn't think so.

I got out of bed, flipped pages in my notebook, picked up the phone again. When the hotel operator came on I read off a number to him. He put the call through and I listened as it rang twice.

A women answered it. Same woman who'd just told me to leave the dead alone. I'd heard her voice once before that, and remembered it now.

I had nothing to say to her that wouldn't wait a day or two. Without saying anything, I replaced the receiver and went back to bed.

ELEVEN

After breakfast the next day I called Charles London's office. He hadn't come in yet. I gave my name and said I'd call later.

I spent another dime calling Frank Fitzroy at the Thirteenth Precinct. "Scudder," I said. "Where are they holding Pinell?"

"They had him downtown. Then I think they shunted him out to Rikers Island. Why?"

"I'd like to see him. What are my chances?"

"Not good."

"You could go out there," I suggested. "I could just be a fellow officer along for the ride."

"I don't know, Matt."

"You'd get something for your time."

"That's not it. Believe me. Thing is, this fucker fell in our laps and I'd hate to see him walk on a technicality. We ring in an unauthorized visitor and his lawyer gets wind of it and gets a wild hair up his ass and it could screw up the whole case. You follow me?"

"It doesn't seem very likely."

"Maybe not, but it's a chance I'm in no rush to take. What do you want from him, anyway?"

"I don't know."

"Maybe I could ask him a question or two for you. Assuming I could get to see him, which I'm not sure I could. His lawyer may have cut off the flow. But if you've got a specific question—"

I was in the phone booth in my hotel lobby and someone was knocking on the door. I told Frank to hang on for a second and opened the door a crack. It was Vinnie, the desk man, to tell me I had a call. I asked who it was and he said it was a woman and she hadn't given her name. I wondered if it was the same one who'd called last night.

I told him to switch it to the house phone and I'd take it in a minute. I uncovered the mouthpiece of the phone I was holding and told Frank I couldn't think of anything in particular that I wanted to ask Louis Pinell, but that I'd keep his offer in mind. He asked if I was getting anyplace with my investigation.

"I don't know," I said. "It's hard to tell. I'm putting in the hours."

"Giving what's-his-name his money's worth. London."

"I suppose so. I have a feeling most of it is wasted motion."

"It's always that way, isn't it? There's days when I figure I must waste ninety percent of my time. But you have to do that to come up with the ten percent that's not a waste."

"That's a point."

"Even if you could see Pinell, that'd be part of the wasted ninety percent. Don't you think?"

"Probably."

I finished up with him, went over to the desk and picked up the house phone. It was Anita.

She said, "Matt? I just wanted to tell you that the check came."

"That's good. I'm sorry it's not more."

"It came at a good time."

I sent money for her and the boys when I had it to send. She never called just to say it had arrived.

I asked how the boys were.

"They're fine," she said. "Of course they're in school now."

"Of course."

"I guess it's been a while since you've seen them."

I felt a little red pinprick of anger. Had she called just to tell me that? Just to push a little guilt button? "I'm on a case," I said. "Soon as it's finished, whenever that is, maybe they can come in and we'll catch a game at the Garden. Or a boxing match."

"They'd like that."

"So would I." I thought of Jan, relieved that her kids were on the other side of the country, relieved she didn't have to visit them anymore, and guilty over her relief. "I'd like that very much," I said.

"Matt, the reason I called—"

"Yes?"

"Oh, God," she said. She sounded sad and tired. "It's Bandy," she said.

"Bandy?"

"The dog. You remember Bandy."

"Of course. What about him?"

"Oh, it's sad," she said. "The vet said he ought to be put to sleep. He said there's really nothing to be done for him at this point."

"Oh," I said. "Well, I suppose if that's what has to be done—"

"I already had him put to sleep. On Friday."

"Oh."

"I guess I thought you would want to know."

"Poor Bandy," I said. "He must have been twelve years old."

"He was fourteen."

"I didn't realize he was that old. That's a long life for a dog."

"It's supposed to be the equivalent of ninety-eight for a human being."

"What was the matter with him?"

"The vet said he just wore out. His kidneys were in bad shape. And he was almost blind. You knew that, didn't you?"

"No."

"For the past year or two his eyesight was failing. It was so sad, Matt. The boys sort of lost interest in him. I think that was the saddest part. They loved him when they were younger but they grew up and he got old and they lost interest." She started to cry. I stood there and held the phone to my ear and didn't say anything.

She said, "I'm sorry, Matt."

"Don't be silly."

"I called you because I wanted to tell somebody and who else could I tell? Do you remember when we got him?"

"I remember."

"I wanted to call him Bandit because of his facial markings, his mask. You said something about give-a-dog-a-bad-name, but we were already calling him Bandy. So we decided it was short for Bandersnatch."

"From *Alice in Wonderland*."

"The vet said he didn't feel anything. He just went to sleep. He took care of disposing of the body for me."

"That's good."

"He had a good life, don't you think? And he was a good dog. He was such a clown. He could always break me up."

She talked for a few more minutes. The conversation just wore out, like the dog. She thanked me again for the check and I said again that I wished it could have been more. I told her to tell the boys I'd be seeing them as soon as I was finished with my current case. She said she'd be sure to tell them. I hung up the phone and went outside.

The sun was screened by clouds and there was a chill wind blowing. Two doors down from the hotel is a bar called McGovern's. They open early.

I went in. The place was empty except for two old men, one behind the bar, one in front of it. The bartender's hand trembled slightly as he poured me a double shot of Early Times and backed it up with a glass of water.

I hoisted the glass, wondered at the wisdom of paying an early visit to London's office with bourbon on my breath, then decided it was a pardonable eccentricity in an unofficial private detective. I thought about poor old Bandy, but of course I wasn't really thinking about the dog. For me, and probably for Anita, he was one of the few threads that had still linked us. Rather like the marriage, he'd taken his sweet time dying.

I drank the drink and got out of there.

London's office was on the sixteenth floor of a twenty-eight-story building on Pine Street. I shared the elevator with two men in forest-green work clothing. One carried a clipboard, the other a tool kit. Neither spoke, nor did I.

I felt like a rat in a maze by the time I found London's office. His name was the first of four lettered on the frosted glass door. Inside, a receptionist with a slight British accent invited me to have a seat, then spoke quietly into a telephone. I looked at a copy of *Sports Illustrated* until a door opened and Charles London beckoned me into his private office.

It was a fair-sized room, comfortable without being luxurious. There was a view of the harbor from his window, only partially blocked by surrounding buildings. We stood on either side of his desk, and I sensed something in the air between us. For a moment I regretted that bourbon at McGovern's, then realized it had nothing to do with the screen that seemed to separate us.

"I wish you'd called," he said. "You'd have been able to save a trip down here."

"I called and they told me you hadn't come in yet."

"I got a message that you would call later."

"I thought I'd save a call."

He nodded. His outfit looked the same as he'd worn to Armstrong's, except that the tie was different. I'm sure the suit and shirt were different, too. He probably had six identical suits, and two drawers of white shirts.

He said, "I'm going to have to ask you to drop the case, Mr. Scudder."

"Oh?"

"You seem unsurprised."

"I picked up the vibration walking in here. Why?"

"My reasons aren't important."

"They are to me."

He shrugged. "I made a mistake," he said. "I sent you on a fool's errand. It was a waste of money."

"You already wasted the money. You might as well let me give you something for it. I can't give it back because I already spent it."

"I wasn't expecting a refund."

"And I didn't come here to ask for any additional money. So what are you saving by telling me to drop the case?"

The pale blue eyes blinked twice behind the rimless glasses. He asked me if I wouldn't sit down. I said I was comfortable standing. He remained standing himself.

He said, "I behaved foolishly. Seeking vengeance, retribution. Troubling the waters. Either that man killed her or some other maniac did and there's probably no way we'll ever know for sure. I was wrong to set you to work raking up the past and disturbing the present."

"Is that what I've been doing?"

"I beg your pardon?"

"Raking up the past and disturbing the present? Maybe that's a good definition of my role. When did you decide to call me off?"

"That's not important."

"Ettinger got to you, didn't he? It must have been yesterday. Saturday's a busy day at the store, they sell a lot of tennis rackets. He probably called you last night, didn't he?" When he hesitated I said, "Go ahead. Tell me it's not important."

"It's not. More to the point, it's not your business, Mr. Scudder."

"I got a wake-up call around one thirty last night from the second Mrs. Ettinger. Did she give you a call about the same time?"

"I don't know what you're talking about."

"She's got a distinctive voice. I heard it the day before when I called Ettinger at home and she told me he was at the Hicksville store. She called last night to tell me to let the dead stay buried. That seems to be what you want, too."

"Yes," he said. "That's what I want."

I picked a paperweight from the top of his desk. An inch-long brass label identified it as a piece of petrified wood from the Arizona desert.

"I can understand what Karen Ettinger's afraid of. Her husband might turn out to be the killer, and that would really turn her world upside down. You'd think a woman in her position would want to know one way or the other. How comfortable could she be from here on in, living with a man she half-suspects of killing his first wife? But people are funny that way. They can push things out of their minds. Whatever happened was years ago and in Brooklyn. And the wench is dead, right? People move and their lives change, so there's nothing for her to worry about, is there?"

He didn't say anything. His paperweight had a piece of black felt on its bottom to keep it from scratching his desk. I replaced it, felt-side down.

I said, "You wouldn't be worried about Ettinger's world, or his wife's world. What's it to you if they get hassled a little? Unless Ettinger had a way to put pressure on you, but I don't think that's it. I don't think you'd be all that easy to push around."

"Mr. Scudder—"

"It's something else, but what? Not money, not a physical threat. Oh, hell, I know what it is."

He avoided my eyes.

"Her reputation. You're afraid of what I'll find in the grave with her. Ettinger must have told you she was having an affair. He told me she wasn't, but I don't think he's that deeply committed to the truth. As a matter of fact, it does look as though she was seeing a man. Maybe more than one man. That may go against the grain of your sense of propriety, but it doesn't weigh too much against the fact that she was murdered. She may have been killed by a lover. She may have been killed by her husband. There are all sorts of possibilities but you don't want to look at any of them because in the course of it the world might find out that your daughter wasn't a virgin."

For a moment I thought he was going to lose his temper. Then something went out of his eyes. "I'm afraid I'll have to ask you to leave now," he said. "I have some calls to make and I have an appointment scheduled in fifteen minutes."

"I guess Mondays are busy in insurance. Like Saturdays in sporting goods."

"I'm sorry that you're embittered. Perhaps later you'll appreciate my position, but—"

"Oh, I appreciate your position," I said. "Your daughter was killed for no reason by a madman and you adjusted to that reality. Then you had a new reality to adjust to, and that turned out to mean coming to grips with the possibility that someone had a reason to kill her, and that it might be a good reason." I shook my head, impatient with myself for talking too much. "I came here to pick up a picture of your daughter," I said. "I don't suppose you happened to bring it."

"Why would you want it?"

"Didn't I tell you the other day?"

"But you're off the case now," he said. He might have been explained something to a slow child. "I don't expect a refund, but I want you to discontinue your investigation."

"You want to fire me."

"If you'd prefer to put it that way."

"But you never hired me in the first place. So how can you fire me?"

"Mr. Scudder –"

"When you open up a can of worms you can't just decide to stuff the worms back in the can. There are a lot of things I set in motion and I want to see where they lead. I'm not going to stop now."

He had an odd look on his face, as though he was a little bit afraid of me. Maybe I'd raised my voice, or looked somehow menacing.

"Relax," I told him. "I won't be disturbing the dead. The dead are beyond disturbance. You had a right to ask me to drop the case and I've got the right to tell you to go to hell. I'm a private citizen pursuing an unofficial investigation. I could do it more efficiently if I had your help, but I can get along without it."

"I wish you'd let it go."

"And I wish you'd back me up. And wishes aren't horses, not for either of us. I'm sorry this isn't turning out the way you wanted it to. I tried to tell you that might be the case. I guess you didn't want to listen."

—

On the way down, the elevator stopped at almost every floor. I went out to the street. It was still overcast, and colder than I remembered it. I walked a block and a half until I found a bar. I had a quick double bourbon and left. A few blocks further along I stopped at another bar and had another drink.

I found a subway, headed for the uptown platform, then changed my mind and waited for a train bound for Brooklyn. I got out at Jay Street and walked up one street and down another and wound up in Boerum Hill. I stopped at a Pentecostal church on Schermerhorn. The bulletin board was full of notices in Spanish. I sat there for a few minutes, hoping things would sort themselves out in my mind, but it didn't work. I found my thoughts bouncing back and forth among dead things—a dead dog, a dead marriage, a dead woman in her kitchen, a dead trail.

A balding man wearing a sleeveless sweater over a maroon shirt asked me something in Spanish. I suppose he wanted to know if he could help me. I got up and left.

I walked around some more. A curious thing, I thought, was that I felt somehow more committed to the pursuit of Barbara Ettinger's killer than I had before her father fired me. It was still as hopeless a quest as it had ever been, doubly hopeless now that I wouldn't even have the cooperation of my client. And yet I seemed to believe what I had said to him about forces having been set in motion. The dead were indeed beyond disturbance, but I had set about disturbing the living and sensed that it would lead somewhere.

I thought of poor old Bandersnatch, always game to chase a stick or go for a walk. He'd bring one of his toys to you to signal his eagerness to play. If you just stood there he'd drop it at your feet, but if you tried to take it away from him he'd set his jaw and hang on grimly.

Maybe I'd learned it from him.

I went to the building on Wyckoff Street. I rang Donald Gilman and Rolfe Waggoner's bell. They weren't in. Neither was Judy Fairborn. I walked on past the building where Jan had lived with—what was his name? Edward. Eddie.

I stopped at a bar and had a drink. Just a straight shot of bourbon, not a double. Just a little something, maintenance drinking against the chill in the air.

I decided I was going to see Louis Pinell. For one thing, I'd ask him if he used a different icepick each time he killed. The autopsies hadn't indicated anything one way or the other. Perhaps forensic medicine isn't that highly developed yet.

I wondered where he got the icepicks. An icepick struck me as a damned old-fashioned instrument. What would you ever use it for outside of murder? People didn't have iceboxes any more, didn't have blocks of ice brought by the iceman. They filled trays with water to make ice cubes or had a gadget in their refrigerator that produced the cubes automatically.

Our refrigerator in Syosset had had an automated ice maker.

Where did you get an icepick? How much did they cost? I was suddenly full of icepick questions. I walked around, found a five-and-ten, asked a clerk in the housewares department where I'd find an icepick. She shunted me to the hardware department, where another clerk told me they didn't carry icepicks.

"I guess they're out of date," I said.

She didn't bother to answer. I walked around some more, stopped at a storefront that sold hardware and kitchen things. The fellow behind the counter was wearing a camel-hair cardigan and chewing the stub of a cigar. I asked if he carried icepicks and he turned without a word and came back with one stapled to a piece of cardboard.

"Ninety-eight cents," he said. "Is one-oh-six with the tax."

I didn't really want it. I had just wondered at price and availability. I paid for it anyway. Outside I stopped at a wire trash basket and discarded the brown paper bag and the piece of cardboard and examined my purchase. The blade was four or five inches long, the point sharp. The handle was a cylinder of dark wood. I held it alternately in one hand and then the other, dropped it back in my pocket.

I went back into the store. The man who'd sold it to me looked up from his magazine. "I just bought that icepick from you," I said.

"Something wrong with it?"

"It's fine. You sell many of them?"

"Some."

"How many?"

"Don't keep track," he said. "Sell one now and then."

"What do people buy them for?"

He gave me the guarded look you get when people begin to wonder about your mental state. "Whatever they want," he said. "I don't guess they pick their teeth with 'em, but anything else they want."

"You been here long?"

"How's that?"

"You had this store a long time?"

"Long enough."

I nodded, left. I didn't ask him who'd bought an icepick from him nine years ago. If I had, he wouldn't have been the only one doubting my sanity. But if someone had asked him that question right after Barbara Ettinger was killed, if someone had asked him and every other housewares and hardware dealer in that part of Brooklyn, and if they'd shown around the appropriate photographs and asked a few other appropriate questions, maybe they would have come up with Barbara's killer then and there.

No reason to do so. No reason to think it was anything but what it looked like, another score for the Icepick Prowler.

I walked around, my hand gripping the butt end of the icepick in my pocket. Handy little thing. You couldn't slash with it, you could only stab, but it would still do a pretty good job on someone.

Was it legal to carry it? The law classified it not as a deadly weapon but as a dangerous instrument. Deadly weapons are things like loaded guns, switch knives, gravity knives, daggers, billies, blackjacks and brass knuckles, articles with no function but murderous assault. An icepick had other uses, though the man who sold it hadn't managed to tell me any of them.

Still, that didn't mean you could carry it legally. A machete's a dangerous instrument in the eyes of the law, not a deadly weapon, but you're not allowed to carry one through the streets of New York.

I took the thing out of my pocket a couple of times and looked at it. Somewhere along the way I dropped it through a sewer grating.

Had the icepick used on Barbara Ettinger vanished the same way? It was possible. It was even possible that it had been dropped down that very sewer grating. All kinds of things were possible.

The wind was getting worse instead of better. I stopped for another drink.

I lost track of the time. At one point I looked at my watch and it was twenty-five minutes of four. I remembered that I was supposed to meet Lynn London at four o'clock. I didn't see how I could get there on time. Still, she was in Chelsea, it wouldn't take all that long –

Then I caught myself. What was I worrying about? Why break my neck to keep an appointment when she wouldn't be keeping it herself? Because her father would have talked to her, either early that morning or late the night before, and she'd know by now that there'd been a change in the London family policy. Matthew Scudder was no longer representing the best interests of the Londons. He was persisting in his folly for reasons of his own, and perhaps he had the right to do this, but he couldn't count on the cooperation of Charles London or his schoolmarm daughter.

"You say something?"

I looked up, met the warm brown eyes of the bartender. "Just talking to myself," I said.

"Nothin' wrong with that."

I liked his attitude. "Might as well give me another," I
said. "And take something for yourself while you're at
it."

I called Jan twice from Brooklyn and her line was busy
both times. When I got back to Manhattan I called her
again from Armstrong's and got another busy signal. I
finished a cup of coffee with a shot in it and tried her
again and the line was still busy.

I had the operator check the line. She came back and
told me the receiver was off the hook. There's a way they
can make the phone ring even if you've taken it off the
hook, and I thought about identifying myself as a policeman and getting her to do that, but decided to let it
go.

I had no right to interrupt the woman. Maybe she was
asleep. Maybe she had company.

Maybe there was a man there, or a woman. It was no
business of mine.

Something settled in my stomach and glowed there
like a hot coal. I had another cup of bourbon-flavored
coffee to drown it.

The evening hurried on by. I didn't really pay it too
much attention. My mind tended to drift.

I had things to think about.

At one point I found myself on the phone, dialing
Lynn London's number. No answer. Well, she'd told me
she had tickets for a concert. And I couldn't remember
why I was calling her, anyway. I'd already decided there

was no point. That was why I'd missed my appointment with her.

Not that she'd have shown up herself. Would have left me standing there, feeling stupid.

So I called Jan again. Still busy.

I thought about going over there. Wouldn't take too long by cab. But what was the point? When a woman takes her phone off the hook it's not because she's hoping you'll come knock on her door.

Hell with her.

Back at the bar, somebody was talking about the First Avenue Slasher. I gathered he was still at large. One of the surviving victims had described how the man had attempted to start a conversation with him before showing his weapon and attacking.

I thought about the little article I'd read about muggers asking you the time or directions. Don't talk to strangers, I thought.

"That's the trouble with this place tonight," I said. "Too many strangers."

A couple of people looked at me. From behind the bar, Billie asked me if I was all right.

"I'm fine," I assured him. "Just that it's too crowded tonight. No room to breathe."

"Probably a good night to turn in early."

"You said it."

But I didn't feel like turning in, just like getting the hell out of there. I went around the corner to McGovern's and had a quick one. The place was dead so I didn't hang around. I hit Polly's Cage across the street and left when the jukebox started getting on my nerves.

The air outside was bracing. It struck me that I'd been drinking all day and that it added up to a hell of a lot of booze, but I seemed to be handling it fine. It wasn't affecting me at all. I was wide awake, clear-minded, clear-headed. It'd be hours before I'd be able to sleep.

I circled the block, stopped at a hole in the wall on Eighth Avenue, stopped again at Joey Farrell's. I felt restless and combative and got out of there when the bartender said something that irritated me. I don't remember what it was.

Then I was walking. I was on Ninth Avenue across the street from Armstrong's, walking south, and there was something hanging in the air that was putting me on my guard. Even as I was wondering at the feeling, a young man stepped out of a doorway ten yards ahead of me.

He had a cigarette in one hand. As I approached he moved purposefully into my path and asked me for a match.

That's how the bastards do it. One stops you and sizes you up. The other moves in behind you, and you get a forearm across the windpipe, a knife at your throat.

I don't smoke but I generally have a pack of matches in my pocket. I cupped my hands, scratched a match. He tucked the unlit cigarette between his lips and leaned forward, and I flipped the burning match in his face and went in under it, grabbing and shoving hard, sending him reeling into the brick wall behind him.

I whirled myself, ready for his partner.

There was nobody behind me. Nothing but an empty street.

That made it simpler. I kept turning, and I was facing him when he came off the wall with his eyes wide and his mouth open. He was my height but lighter in build, late teens or early twenties, uncombed dark hair and a face white as paper in the light of the streetlamps.

I moved in quick and hit him in the middle. He swung at me and I sidestepped the punch and hit him again an inch or two above his belt buckle. That brought his hands down and I swung my right forearm in an arc and hit him in the mouth with my elbow. He drew back and clapped both hands to his mouth.

I said, "Turn around and grab that wall! Come on, you fucker. Get your hands on the wall!"

He said I was crazy, that he hadn't done anything. The words came out muffled through the hands he was holding to his mouth.

But he turned around and grabbed the wall.

I moved in, hooked a foot in front of his, drew his foot back so that he couldn't come off the wall in a hurry.

"I didn't do nothing," he said. "What's the matter with you?"

I told him to put his head against the wall.

"All I did was ask you for a match."

I told him to shut up. I frisked him and he stood still for it. A little blood trickled from the corner of his mouth. Nothing serious. He was wearing one of those leather jackets with a pile collar and two big pockets in front. Bomber jackets, I think they call them. The pocket on the left held a wad of Kleenex and a pack of Winston Lights. The other pocket held a knife. A flick of my wrist and the blade dropped into place.

A gravity knife. One of the seven deadly weapons.

"I just carry it," he said.

"For what?"

"Protection."

"From who? Little old ladies:"

I took a wallet off his hip. He had ID that indicated he was Anthony Sforczak and he lived in Woodside, Queens. I said, "You're a long ways from home, Tony."

"So?"

He had two tens and some singles in his wallet. In another pants pocket I found a thick roll of bills secured by a rubber band, and in the breast pocket of his shirt, under the leather jacket, I found one of those disposable butane lighters.

"It's out of fluid," he said.

I flicked it. Flame leaped from it and I showed it to him. The heat rose and he jerked his head to the side. I released the thumbcatch and the flame died.

"It was out before. Wouldn't light."

"So why keep it? Why not throw it away?"

"It's against the law to litter."

"Turn around."

He came off the wall slowly, eyes wary. A little line of blood trailed from the corner of his mouth down over his chin. His mouth was starting to puff up some where my elbow had caught him.

He wouldn't die of it.

I gave him the wallet and the cigarette lighter. I tucked the roll of bills in my own pocket.

"That's my money," he said.

"You stole it."

"Like hell I did! What are you gonna do, keep it?"

"What do you think?" I flicked the knife open and held it so that the light glinted off the face of the blade. "You better not turn up in this part of the city again. Another thing you better not do is carry a blade when half the department's looking for the First Avenue Slasher."

He stared at me. Something in his eyes said he wished I didn't have that knife in my hand. I met his gaze and closed the knife, dropped it on the ground behind me.

"Go ahead," I said. "Be my guest."

I balanced on the balls of my feet, waiting for him. For a moment he might have been considering it, and I was hoping he'd make a move. I could feel the blood singing in my veins, pulsing in my temples.

He said, "You're crazy, you know? What you are is crazy," and he edged off ten or twenty yards, then half-ran to the corner.

I stood watching until he was out of sight.

The street was still empty. I found the gravity knife on the pavement and put it in my pocket. Across the street, Armstrong's door opened and a young man and woman emerged. They walked down the street holding hands.

I felt fine. I wasn't drunk. I'd had a day of maintenance drinking, nothing more. Look how I'd handled the punk. Nothing wrong with my instincts, nothing slow about my reflexes. The booze wasn't getting in the way. Just a matter of taking on fuel, of keeping a full tank. Nothing wrong with that.

TWELVE

I came suddenly awake. There was no warm-up period. It was as abrupt as turning on a transistor radio.

I was on my bed in my hotel room, lying on top of the covers with my head on the pillow. I had piled my clothes on the chair but slept in my underwear. There was a foul taste in my dry mouth and I had a killer headache.

I got up. I felt shaky and awful, and a sense of impending doom hung in the air, as though if I turned around quickly I could look Death in the eye.

I didn't want a drink but knew I needed one to take the edge off the way I felt. I couldn't find the bourbon bottle until it finally turned up in the waste basket. Evidently I'd finished it before I went to bed. I wondered how much it had contained.

No matter. It was empty now.

I held out a hand, studied it. No visible tremors. I flexed the fingers. Not as steady as Gibraltar, maybe, but not a case of the shakes, either.

Shaky inside, though.

I couldn't remember returning to the hotel. I probed gingerly at my memory and couldn't get any further than the boy scuttling down the street and around the corner. Anthony Sforczak, that was his name.

See? Nothing wrong with my memory.

Except that it ran out at that point. Or perhaps a moment later, when the young couple came out of Armstrong's and walked up the street holding hands. Then it all went blank, coming into focus again with me coming to in my hotel room. What time was it, anyway?

My watch was still on my wrist. Quarter after nine. And it was light outside my window, so that meant a.m. Not that I really had to look to be sure. I hadn't lost a day, just the length of time it took me to walk half a block home and get to bed.

Assuming I'd come straight home.

I stripped off my underwear and got into the shower. While I was under the spray I could hear my phone ringing. I let it ring. I spent a long time under the hot spray, then took a blast of cold for as long as I could stand it, which wasn't very long. I toweled dry and shaved. My hand wasn't as steady as it might have been but I took my time and didn't cut myself.

I didn't like what I saw in the mirror. A lot of red in the eyes. I thought of Havermeyer's description of Susan Potowski, her eyes swimming in blood. I didn't like my red eyes, or the mesh of broken blood vessels on my cheekbones and across the bridge of my nose.

I knew what put them there. Drink put them there. Nothing else. I could forget about what it might be doing to my liver because my liver was tucked away where I didn't have to look at it every morning.

And where nobody else could see it.

I got dressed, put on all clean clothes, stuffed everything else in my laundry bag. The shower helped and the shave helped and the clean clothes helped, but in spite of all three I could feel remorse settling over my shoulders like a cape. I didn't want to look at the previous night because I knew I wasn't going to like what I'd see there.

But what choice did I have?

I put the roll of bills in one pocket, the gravity knife in the other. I went downstairs and out, walking past the desk without breaking stride. I knew there'd be messages there but I figured they'd keep.

I decided not to stop at McGovern's but when I got there I turned in. Just one quick drink to still the invisible shaking. I drank it like the medicine it was.

Around the corner I sat in a rear pew at St. Paul's. For what seemed like a long time I didn't even think. I just sat there.

Then the thoughts started. No way to stop them, really.

I'd been drunk the night before and hadn't known it. I'd probably been drunk fairly early in the day. There were patches in Brooklyn that I couldn't remember clearly, and I didn't seem to have any recollection of the subway ride back to Manhattan. For that matter, I couldn't be sure I'd ridden the subway. I might have taken a cab.

I remembered talking to myself in a Brooklyn bar. I must have been drunk then. I didn't tend to talk to myself when I was sober.

Not yet, anyway.

All right, I could live with all that. I drank too goddamn much, and when you do that with consistency there are going to be times when you get drunk without wanting to. This wasn't the first time and I didn't suspect it would be the last. It came with the territory.

But I'd been drunk when I was playing Hero Cop on Ninth Avenue, drunk with the booze for high-octane fuel. My street-smart instincts that warned me about a mugging were less a source of pride the morning after.

Maybe he just wanted a match.

My gorge rose at the thought and I tasted bile at the back of my throat. Maybe he was just another kid from Woodside having himself a night on the town. Maybe he'd been a mugger only in my mind, my drunken mind. Maybe I'd beaten him and robbed him for no good reason at all.

But he'd asked for a match when he had a working lighter.

So? That was an icebreaker as old as tobacco. Ask for a match, strike up a conversation. He could have been a male hustler. He would hardly have been the first gay man to put on a bomber jacket.

He was carrying a gravity knife.

So? Frisk the city and you could stock an arsenal. Half the city was carrying something to protect it from the other half. The knife was a deadly weapon and he was breaking a law carrying it, but it didn't prove anything.

He knew how to grab that wall. It wasn't his first frisk.

And that didn't prove anything either. There are neighborhoods where you can't grow up without getting stopped and tossed once a week by the cops.

And the money? The roll of bills?

He could have come by it honestly. Or he could have earned it in any of innumerable dishonest ways and still not have been a mugger.

And my vaunted cop instincts? Hell, the minute he came out of the doorway I'd known he was going to approach me.

Right. And I'd also known his partner was moving in behind me, knew it as if I'd had eyes in the back of my head. Except there was nobody there. So much for the infallibility of instinct.

I took out the gravity knife, opened it. Suppose I'd been carrying it the night before. More realistically, suppose I'd still been carrying the icepick I'd bought in Boerum Hill. Would I have limited myself to a couple of body punches and a forearm smash to the face? Or would I have worked with the materials at hand?

I felt shaky, and it was more than the hangover.

I closed the knife and put it away. I took out the roll of bills, removed the rubber band, counted the cash. I made it a hundred and seventy dollars in five and tens.

If he was a mugger, why didn't he have the knife in his hand? How come it was in his jacket pocket with the flap buttoned down?

Or *was* the flap buttoned?

Didn't matter. I sorted the money and added it to my own. On my way out I lit a couple of candles, then slipped seventeen dollars into the poor box.

At the corner of Fifty-seventh I dropped the gravity knife into a sewer.

THIRTEEN

My cab driver was an Israeli immigrant and I don't think he'd ever heard of Rikers Island. I told him to follow the signs for LaGuardia airport. When we got close I gave him directions. I got out at a luncheonette at the foot of the bridge that spans Bowery Bay and the channel of the East River that separates the island from the rest of Queens.

Lunch hour had come and gone and the place was mostly empty. A few men in work clothes were seated at the counter. About halfway down a man sat in a booth with a cup of coffee and looked up expectantly at my approach. I introduced myself and he said he was Marvin Hiller.

"My car's outside," he said. "Or did you want to grab a cup of coffee? The only thing is I'm a little bit rushed. I had a long morning in Queens Criminal Court and I'm supposed to be at my dentist's in forty-five minutes. If I'm late I'm late."

I told him I didn't care about coffee. He paid his tab and we went outside and rode his car over the bridge. He was a pleasant and rather earnest man a few years younger than I and he looked like what he was, a lawyer with an office on Queens Boulevard in Elmhurst. One of his clients, one who'd be contributing very little toward the rent on that office, was Louis Pinell.

I'd gotten his name from Frank Fitzroy and managed to get his secretary to beep him and call me at the hotel. I'd expected a flat turndown on my request for clearance to see Pinell and got just the reverse. "Just so it's kosher," he had said, "why don't you meet me out there and we'll drive over together. You'll probably get more out of him that way. He's a little more comfortable about talking with his lawyer present."

Now he said, "I don't know what you'll be able to get from him. I suppose you mostly want to satisfy yourself that he didn't kill the Ettinger woman."

"I suppose."

"I would think he's in the clear on that one. The evidence is pretty clear-cut. If it was just his word I'd say forget it, because who knows what they remember and what they make up when they're as crazy as he is."

"He's really crazy?"

"Oh, he's a bedbug," Hiller said. "No question about it. You'll see for yourself. I'm his attorney, but between ourselves I see my job as a matter of making sure he never gets out without a leash. It's a good thing I drew this case."

"Why's that?"

"Because anybody crazy enough to want to could get him off without a whole lot of trouble. I'm going to plead him, but if I made a fight the State's case wouldn't stand up. All they've got is his confession and you could knock that out a dozen different ways, including that he was cuckoo at the time he confessed. They've got no evidence, not after nine years. There's lawyers who think the advocate system means they should go to bat for a guy like Lou and put him back on the streets."

"He'd do it again."

"Of course he'd do it again. He had a fucking icepick in his pocket when they collared him. Again between ourselves, I think lawyers with that attitude ought to be in jail alongside their clients. But in the meantime here I am, playing God. What do you want to ask Lou?"

"There was another Brooklyn killing. I might ask him a few questions about that."

"Sheepshead Bay. He copped to that one."

"That's right. I don't know what else I'll ask him. I'm probably wasting my time. And yours."

"Don't worry about it."

Thirty or forty minutes later we were driving back to the mainland and I was apologizing again for wasting his time.

"You did me a favor," he said. "I'm going to have to make another dentist's appointment. You ever have periodontal surgery?"

"No."

"You're a wise man. This guy's my wife's cousin and he's pretty good, but what they do is they carve your gums. They do a section of your mouth at a time. Last time I went I wound up taking codeine every four hours for a week. I walked around in this perpetual fog. I suppose it's worth it in the long run, but don't feel you took me away from something enjoyable."

"If you say so."

I told him he could drop me anywhere but he insisted on giving me a lift to the subway stop at Northern Boulevard. On the way we talked a little about Pinell. "You can see why they picked him up on the street," he said. "That craziness is right there in his eyes. One look and you see it."

"There are a lot of street crazies."

"But he's dangerous-crazy and it shows. And yet I'm never nervous in his presence. Well, I'm not a woman and he hasn't got an icepick. That might have something to do with it."

At the subway entrance I got out of the car and hesitated for a moment, and he leaned toward me, one arm over the back of the seat. We both seemed reluctant to take leave of each other. I liked him and sensed that he held me in similar regard.

"You're not licensed," he said. "Isn't that what you said?"

"That's right."

"Couldn't you get a license?"

"I don't want one."

"Well, maybe I could throw some work your way all the same, if the right sort of thing came along."

"Why would you want to?"

"I don't know. I liked your manner with Lou. And I get the feeling with you that you think the truth is important." He chuckled. "Besides, I owe you. You spared me a half-hour in the dentist's chair."

"Well, if I ever need a lawyer—"

"Right. You know who to call."

—

I just missed a Manhattan-bound train. While I waited for the next one on the elevated platform I managed to find a phone in working order and tried Lynn London's number. I'd checked the hotel desk before I called Hiller, and there'd been a message from her the night before, probably wondering why I hadn't shown up. I wondered if she'd been the one who called during my shower. Whoever it was hadn't elected to leave a message. The desk man said the caller had been a woman, but I'd learned not to count too heavily on his powers of recollection.

Lynn's number didn't answer. No surprise. She was probably still in school, or on her way home. Had she mentioned any afternoon plans? I couldn't remember.

I retrieved my dime, started to put it and my notebook away. Was there anyone else I should call? I flipped pages in my notebook, struck by how many names and numbers and addresses I'd written down, considering how little I'd managed to accomplish.

Karen Ettinger? I could ask her what she was afraid of. Hiller had just told me he sensed that I thought the truth was important. Evidently she thought it was worth hiding.

It'd be a toll call, though. And I didn't have much change.

Charles London? Frank Fitzroy? An ex-cop on the Upper West Side? His ex-wife on the Lower East Side?

Mitzi Pomerance? Jan Keane?

Probably still had the phone off the hook.

I put the notebook away, and the dime. I could have used a drink. I'd had nothing since that one eye-opener at McGovern's. I'd eaten a late breakfast since then, had drunk several cups of coffee, but that was it.

I looked over the low wall at the rear of the platform. My eye fastened on red neon in a tavern window. I'd just missed a train. I could have a quick one and be back in plenty of time for the next one.

I sat down on a bench and waited for my train.

I changed trains twice and wound up at Columbus Circle. The sky was darkening by the time I hit the street, turning that particular cobalt blue that it gets over New York. There were no messages waiting for me at my hotel. I called Lynn London from the lobby.

This time I reached her. "The elusive Mr. Scudder," she said. "You stood me up."

"I'm sorry."

"I waited for you yesterday afternoon. Not for long, because I didn't have too much time available. I suppose something came up, but you didn't call, either."

I remembered how I had considered keeping the appointment and how I'd decided against it. Alcohol had made the decision for me. I'd been in a warm bar and it was cold outside.

"I'd just spoken to your father," I said. "He asked me to drop the case. I figured he'd have been in touch with you to tell you not to cooperate with me."

"So you just decided to write off the Londons, is that it?" There was a trace of amusement in her voice. "I was here waiting, as I said. Then I went out and kept my date for the evening, and when I got home my father called.

To tell me he'd ordered you off the case but that you intended to persist with it all the same."

So I could have seen her. Alcohol had made the decision, and had made it badly.

"He told me not to offer you any encouragement. He said he'd made a mistake raking up the past to begin with."

"But you called me. Or was that before you spoke to him?"

"Once before and once after. The first call was because I was angry with you for standing me up. The second call was because I was angry with my father."

"Why?"

"Because I don't like being told what to do. I'm funny that way. He says you wanted a picture of Barbara. I gather he refused to give it to you. Do you still want one?"

Did I? I couldn't recall now what I'd planned to do with it. Maybe I'd make the rounds of hardware stores, showing it to everyone who sold icepicks.

"Yes," I said. "I still want one."

"Well, I can supply that much. I don't know what else I can give you. But one thing I can't give you at the moment is time. I was on my way out the door when the phone range. I've got my coat on. I'm meeting a friend for dinner, and then I'm going to be busy this evening."

"With group therapy."

"How did you know that? Did I mention it the last time we talked? You have a good memory."

"Sometimes."

"Just let me think. Tomorrow night's also impossible. I'd say come over tonight after therapy but by then I generally feel as though I've been through the wringer. After school tomorrow there's a faculty meeting, and by the time that's over—look, could you come to the school?"

"Tomorrow?"

"I've got a free period from one to two. Do you know where I teach?"

"A private school in the Village, but I don't know which one."

"It's the Devonhurst School. Sounds very preppy, doesn't it? Actually it's anything but. And it's in the East Village. Second Avenue between Tenth and Eleventh. The east side of the street closer to Eleventh than Tenth."

"I'll find it."

"I'll be in Room Forty-one. And Mr. Scudder? I wouldn't want to be stood up a second time."

I went around the corner to Armstrong's. I had a hamburger and a small salad, then some bourbon in coffee. They switch bartenders at eight, and when Billie came in a half-hour before his shift started I went over to him.

"I guess I was pretty bad last night," I said.

"Oh, you were okay," he said.

"It was a long day and night."

"You were talking a little loud," he said. "Aside from that you were your usual self. And you knew to leave here and make it an early night."

Except I hadn't made it an early night.

I went back to my table and had another bourbon and coffee. By the time I was finished with it, the last of my hangover was gone. I'd shaken off the headache fairly early on, but the feeling of being a step or two off the pace had persisted throughout the day.

Great system: the poison and the antidote come in the same bottle.

I went to the phone, dropped a dime. I almost dialed Anita's number and sat there wondering why. I didn't want to talk about a dead dog, and that was as close as we'd come to a meaningful conversation in years.

I dialed Jan's number. My notebook was in my pocket but I didn't have to get it out. The number was just right there at hand.

"It's Matthew," I said. "I wondered if you felt like company."

"Oh."

"Unless you're busy."

"No, I'm not. As a matter of fact, I'm a little under the weather. I was just settling in for a quiet evening in front of the television set."

"Well, if you'd rather be alone—"

"I didn't say that." There was a pause. "I wouldn't want to make it a late evening."

"Neither would I."

"You remember how to get here?"

"I remember."

On the way there I felt like a kid on a date. I rang her bell according to the code and stood at the curb. She tossed me the key. I went inside and rode up in the big elevator.

She was wearing a skirt and sweater and had doeskin slippers on her feet. We stood looking at each other for a moment and then I handed her the paper bag I was carrying. She took out the two bottles, one of Teacher's Scotch, the other of the brand of Russian vodka she favored.

"The perfect hostess gift," she said. "I thought you were a bourbon drinker."

"Well, it's a funny thing. I had a clear head the other morning, and it occurred to me that Scotch might be less likely to give me a hangover."

She put the bottles down. "I wasn't going to drink tonight," she said.

"Well, it'll keep. Vodka doesn't go bad."

"Not if you don't drink it. Let me fix you something. Straight, right?"

"Right."

It was stilted at first. We'd been close to one another, we'd spent a night in bed together, but we were nevertheless stiff and awkward with each other. I started talking about the case, partly because I wanted to talk to someone about it, partly because it was what we had in common. I told her how my client had tried to take me off the case and how I was staying with it anyway. She didn't seem to find this unusual.

Then I talked about Pinell.

"He definitely didn't kill Barbara Ettinger," I said, "and he definitely did commit the icepick murder in Sheepshead Bay. I didn't really have much doubt about either of those points but I wanted to have my own impressions to work with. And I just plain wanted to see him. I wanted some sense of the man."

"What was he like?"

"Ordinary. They're always ordinary, aren't they? Except I don't know that that's the right word for it. The thing about Pinell is that he looked insignificant."

"I think I saw a picture of him in the paper."

"You don't get the full effect from a photograph. Pinell's the kind of person you don't notice. You see guys like him delivering lunches, taking tickets in a movie theater. Slight build, furtive manner, and a face that just won't stay in your memory."

"'The Banality of Evil.'"

"What's that?"

She repeated the phrase. "It's the title of an essay about Adolf Eichmann."

"I don't know that Pinell's evil. He's crazy. Maybe evil's a form of insanity. Anyway, you don't need a psychiatrist's report to know he's crazy. It's right there in his eyes. Speaking of eyes, that's another thing I wanted to ask him."

"What?"

"If he stabbed them all in both eyes. He said he did. He did that right away, before he went to work turning their bodies into pincushions."

She shuddered. "Why?"

"That was the other thing I wanted to ask him. Why the eyes? It turned out he had a perfectly logical reason. He did it to avoid detection."

"I don't follow you."

"He thought a dead person's eyes would retain the last image they perceived before death. If that were the case you could obtain a picture of the murderer by scanning the victim's retina. He was just guarding against this possibility by destroying their eyes."

"Jesus."

"The funny thing is that he's not the first person to have that theory. During the last century some criminologists believed the same thing Pinell hit on. They just figured it was a matter of time before the necessary technology existed for recovering the image from the retina. And who knows that it won't be possible someday? A doctor could give you all sorts of reasons why it'll never be physiologically possible, but look at all the things that would have seemed at least as farfetched a hundred years ago. Or even twenty years ago."

"So Pinell's just a little ahead of his time, is that it?" She got up, carried my empty glass to the bar. She filled it and poured a glass of vodka for herself. "I do believe that calls for a drink. 'Here's looking at you, kid.' That's as close as I can come to an imitation of Humphrey Bogart. I do better with clay."

She sat down and said, "I wasn't going to drink anything today. Well, what the hell."

"I want to go fairly light myself."

She nodded, her eyes aimed at the glass in her hand. "I was glad when you called, Matthew. I didn't think you were going to."

"I tried to get you last night. I kept getting a busy signal."

"I had the phone off the hook."

"I know."

"You had them check it? I just wanted to keep the world away last night. When I'm in here with the door locked and the phone off the hook and the shades down, that's when I'm really safe. Do you know what I mean?"

"I think so."

"See, I didn't wake up with a clear head Sunday morning. I got drunk Sunday night. And then I got drunk again last night."

"Oh."

"And then I got up this morning and took a pill to stop the shakes and decided I'd stay away from it for a day or two. Just to get off the roller-coaster, you know?"

"Sure."

"And here I am with a glass in my hand. Isn't that a surprise?"

"You should have said something, Jan. I wouldn't have brought the vodka."

"It's no big deal."

"I wouldn't have brought the Scotch, either. I had too much to drink last night myself. We could be together tonight without drinking."

"You really think so?"

"Of course."

Her large gray eyes looked quite bottomless. She stared sadly at me for a long moment, then brightened. "Well, it's too late to test that hypothesis right now, isn't it? Why don't we just make the best of what we have?"

We didn't do all that much drinking. She had enough vodka to catch up with me and then we both coasted. She played some records and we sat together on the couch and listened to them, not talking much. We started making love on the couch and then went into the bedroom to finish the job.

We were good together, better than we'd been Saturday night. Novelty is a spice, but when the chemistry is good between lovers, familiarity enhances their lovemaking. I got out of myself some, and felt a little of what she felt.

Afterward we went back to the couch and I started talking about the murder of Barbara Ettinger. "She's buried so goddamn deep," I said. "It's not just the amount of time that's gone by. Nine years is a long time, but there are people who died nine years ago and you could walk through their lives and find everything pretty much as they left it. The same people in the houses next door and everybody leading the same kind of life.

"With Barbara, everybody's gone through a sea-change. You closed the day-care center and left your husband and moved here. Your husband took the kids and beat it to California. I was one of the first cops on the scene, and God knows my life turned upside down since then. There were three cops who investigated the case in Sheepshead Bay, or started to. Two of them are dead and one left the force and his wife and lives in a furnished room and stands guard in a department store."

"And Doug Ettinger's remarried and selling sporting goods."

I nodded. "And Lynn London's been married and divorced, and half the neighbors on Wyckoff Street have moved somewhere or other. I know Americans lead mobile lives. I read somewhere that every year twenty percent of the country changes its place of residence. Even so, it's as though every wind on earth's been busy blowing sand on top of her grave. It's like digging for Troy."

"'Deep with the first dead.'"

"How's that?"

"I don't know if I remember it right. Just a second." She crossed the room, searched the bookshelves, removed a slim volume and paged through it. "It's Dylan Thomas," she said, "and it's in here somewhere. Where the hell is it? I'm sure it's in here. Here it is."

She read:

"Deep with the first dead lies London's daughter,
Robed in the long friends,
The grains beyond age, the dark veins of her mother,
Secret by the unmourning water
Of the riding Thames.
After the first death, there is no other."

"London's daughter," I said.

"As in the city of London. But that must be what made me think of it. Deep with the first dead lies Charles London's daughter."

"Read it again."

She did.

"Except there's a door there somewhere if I could just find the handle to it. It wasn't some nut that killed her. It was someone with a reason, someone she knew. Someone who purposely made it look like Pinell's handiwork. And the killer's still around. He didn't die or drop out of sight. He's still around. I don't have any grounds to believe that but it's a feeling I can't shake."

"You think it's Doug?"

"If I don't, I'm the only one who doesn't. Even his wife thinks he did it. She may not know that's what she thinks, but why else is she scared of what I'll find?"

"But you think it's somebody else?"

"I think an awful lot of lives changed radically after her death. Maybe her dying had something to do with those changes. With some of them, anyway."

"Doug's, obviously. Whether he killed her or not."

"Maybe it affected other lives, too."

"Like a stone in a pond? The ripple effect?"

"Maybe. I don't know just what happened or how. I told you, it's a matter of a hunch, a feeling. Nothing concrete that I can point at."

"Your cop instincts, is that it?"

I laughed. She asked what was funny. I said, "It's not so funny. I've had all day to wonder about the validity of my cop instincts."

"How do you mean?"

And so I wound up telling her more than I'd planned. About everything from Anita's phone call to a kid with a gravity knife. Two nights ago I'd found out what a good listener she was, and she was no worse at it this time around.

When I was done she said, "I don't know why you're down on yourself. You could have been killed."

"If it was really a mugging attempt."

"What were you supposed to do, wait until he stuck a knife into you? And why was he carrying a knife in the first place? I don't know what a gravity knife is, but it doesn't sound like something you stick in your pocket in case you need to cut a piece of string."

"He could have been carrying it for protection."

"And the roll of money? It sounds to me as though he's one of those closet cases who pick up gay men and rob them, and sometimes beat them up or kill them while they're at it to prove how straight they are. And you're worrying because you gave a kid like that a bloody lip?"

I shook my head. "I'm worrying because my judgment wasn't sound."

"Because you were drunk."

"And didn't even know it."

"Was your judgment off the night you shot the two holdup men? The night that Puerto Rican girl got killed?"

"You're a pretty sharp lady, aren't you?"

"A fucking genius."

"That's the question, I guess. And the answer is no, it wasn't. I hadn't had all that much to drink and I wasn't feeling it. But—"

"But you got echoes just the same."

"Right."

"And didn't want to look straight at them, any more than Karen Ettinger wants to look straight at the fact that she thinks her husband might have murdered his first wife."

"A very sharp lady."

"They don't come any sharper. Feel better now?"

"Uh-huh."

"Talking helps. But you kept it so far inside you didn't even know it was there." She yawned. "Being a sharp lady is tiring work."

"I can believe it."

"Want to go to bed?"

"Sure."

But I didn't stay the night. I thought I might, but I was still awake when her breathing changed to indicate that she was sleeping. I lay first on one side and then on the other, and it was clear I wasn't ready to sleep. I got out of bed and padded quietly into the other room.

I dressed, then stood at the window and looked out at Lispenard Street. There was plenty of Scotch left but I didn't want to drink any of it.

I let myself out. A block away on Canal Street I managed to flag a cab. I got uptown in time to catch the last half-hour or so at Armstrong's, but I said the hell with it and went straight to my room.

I got to sleep eventually.

FOURTEEN

I had a night of dreams and shallow sleep. The dog, Bandy, turned up in one of the dreams. He wasn't really dead. His death had been faked as part of some elaborate scam. He told me all this, told me too that he'd always been able to talk but had been afraid to disclose this talent. "If I'd only known," I marveled, "what conversations we could have had!"

I awoke refreshed and clearheaded and fiercely hungry. I had bacon and eggs and home fries at the Red Flame and read the *News*. They'd caught the First Avenue Slasher, or at the least had arrested someone they said was the Slasher. A photograph of the suspect bore a startling resemblance to the police artist's sketch that had run earlier. That doesn't happen too often.

I was on my second cup of coffee when Vinnie slid into the booth across from me. "Woman in the lobby," he said.

"For me?"

He nodded. "Young, not bad-looking. Nice clothes, nice hair. Gave me a couple of bucks to point you out when you came in. I don't even know if you're comin' back, so I figured I'd take a chance, look here and there and see if I could find you. I got Eddie coverin' the desk for me. You comin' back to the hotel?"

"I hadn't planned to."

"What you could do, see, you could look her over and gimme a sign to point you out or not point you out. I'd just as soon earn the couple of bucks, but I'm not gonna go and retire on it, you know what I mean? If you want to duck this dame—"

"You can point me out," I said. "Whoever she is."

He went back to the desk. I finished my coffee and the paper and took my time returning to the hotel. When I walked in Vinnie nodded significantly toward the wing chair over by the cigarette machine, but he needn't have bothered. I'd have spotted her without help. She looked utterly out of place, a well-groomed, well-coiffed, color-coordinated suburban princess who'd found her way to the wrong part of Fifty-seventh Street. A few blocks east she might have been having an adventure, making the rounds of the art galleries, looking for a print that would go well with the mushroom-toned drapes in the family room.

I let Vinnie earn his money, strolled past her, stood waiting for the elevator. Its doors were just opening when she spoke my name.

I said, "Hello, Mrs. Ettinger."

"How—"

"Saw your picture on your husband's desk. And I probably would have recognized your voice, although I've only heard it over the phone." The blonde hair was a little longer than in the picture in Douglas Ettinger's photo cube, and the voice in person was less nasal, but there was no mistaking her. "I heard your voice a couple of times. Once when I called you, once when you called me, and again when I called you back."

"I thought that was you," she said. "It frightened me when the phone rang and you didn't say anything."

"I just wanted to make sure I'd recognized the voice."

"I called you since then. I called twice yesterday."

"I didn't get any messages."

"I didn't leave any. I don't know what I'd have said if I reached you. Is there someplace more private where we can talk?"

I took her out for coffee, not to the Red Flame but to another similar place down the block. On the way out Vinnie tipped me a wink and a sly smile. I wonder how much money she'd given him.

Less, I'm sure, than she was prepared to give me. We were no sooner settled with our coffee than she put her purse on the table and gave it a significant tap.

"I have an envelope in here," she announced. "There's five thousand dollars in it."

"That's a lot of cash to be carrying in this town."

"Maybe you'd like to carry it for me." She studied my face, and when I failed to react she leaned forward, dropping her voice conspiratorially. "The money's for you, Mr. Scudder. Just do what Mr. London already asked you to do. Drop the case."

"What are you afraid of, Mrs. Ettinger?"

"I just don't want you poking around in our lives."

"What is it you think I might find there?" Her hand clutched her purse, seeking security in the presumptive power of five thousand dollars. Her nail polish was the color of iron rust. Gently I said, "Do you think your husband killed his first wife?"

"No!"

"Then what have you got to be afraid of?"

"I don't know."

"When did you meet your husband, Mrs. Ettinger?"

She met my eyes, didn't answer.

"Before his wife was killed?" Her fingers kneaded her handbag. "He went to college on Long Island. You're younger than he is, but you could have known him then."

"That was before he even knew her," she said. "Long before they were married. Then we happened to run into each other again after her death."

"And you were afraid I'd find that out?"

"I—"

"You were seeing him before she died, weren't you?"

"You can't prove that."

"Why would I have to prove it? Why would I even want to prove it?"

She opened the purse. Her fingers were clumsy with the clasp but she got the bag open and took out a manila bank envelope. "Five thousand dollars," she said.

"Put it away."

"Isn't it enough? It's a lot of money. Isn't five thousand dollars a lot of money for doing nothing?"

"It's too much. You didn't kill her, did you, Mrs. Ettinger?"

"Me?" She had trouble getting a grip on the question. "Me? Of course not."

"But you were glad when she died."

"That's horrible," she said. "Don't say that."

"You were having an affair with him. You wanted to marry him, and then she was killed. How could you help being glad?"

Her eyes were pitched over my shoulder, gazing off into the distance. Her voice was as remote as her gaze. She said, "I didn't know she was pregnant. He said . . . he said he hadn't known that either. He told me they weren't sleeping together. Having sex, I mean. Of course they slept together, they shared a bed, but he said they weren't having sex. I believed him."

The waitress was approaching to refill our coffee cups. I held up a hand to ward off the interruption. Karen Ettinger said, "He said she was carrying another man's child. Because it couldn't have been his baby."

"Is that what you told Charles London?"

"I never spoke to Mr. London."

"Your husband did, though, didn't he? Is that what he told him? Is that what London was afraid would come out if I stayed on the case?"

Her voice was detached, remote. "He said she was pregnant by another man. A black man. He said the baby would have been black."

"That's what he told London."

"Yes."

"Had he ever told you that?"

"No. I think it was just something he made up to in- fluence Mr. London." She looked at me, and her eyes showed me a little of the person hidden beneath the care- ful suburban exterior. "Just like the rest of it was some- thing he made up for my sake. It was probably his baby."

"You don't think she was having an affair?"

"Maybe. Maybe she was. But she must have been sleeping with him, too. Or else she would have been careful not to get pregnant. Women aren't stupid." She blinked her eyes several times. "Except about some things. Men always tell their girlfriends that they've stopped sleeping with their wives. And it's always a lie."

"Do you think that—"

She rolled right over my question. "He's probably telling her that he's not sleeping with me anymore," she said, her tone very matter-of-fact. "And it's a lie."

"Telling whom?"

"Whoever he's having an affair with."

"Your husband is currently having an affair with someone?"

"Yes," she said, and frowned. "I didn't know that until just now. I knew it, but I didn't know that I knew it. I wish you had never taken this case. I wish Mr. London had never heard of you in the first place."

"Mrs. Ettinger—"

She was standing now, her purse gripped in both hands, her face showing her pain. "I had a good marriage," she insisted. "And what have I got now? Will you tell me that? What have I got now?"

FIFTEEN

I don't suppose she wanted an answer. I certainly didn't
have one for her, and she didn't hang around to find out
what else I might have to say. She walked stiffly out of
the coffee shop. I stayed long enough to finish my own
coffee, then left a tip and paid the check. Not only hadn't
I taken her five thousand dollars, but I'd wound up buying her coffee.

It was a nice day out and I thought I'd kill a little time
by walking part of the way to my appointment with
Lynn London. As it turned out I walked all the way
downtown and east, stopping once to sit on a park bench
and another time for coffee and a roll. When I crossed
Fourteenth Street I ducked into Dan Lynch's and had the
first drink of the day. I'd thought earlier that I might
switch to Scotch, which had once again spared me a
hangover, but I'd ordered a shot of bourbon with a short
beer for a chaser before I remembered my decision. I
drank it down and enjoyed the warmth of it. The saloon

had a rich beery smell and I enjoyed that, too, and would have liked to linger awhile. But I'd already stood up the schoolteacher once.

I found the school, walked in. No one questioned my entering it or stopped me in the corridors. I located Room 41 and stood in the doorway for a moment, studying the woman seated at the blond oak desk. She was reading a book and unaware of my presence. I knocked on the open door and she looked up at me.

"I'm Matthew Scudder," I said.

"And I'm Lynn London. Come in. Close the door."

She stood up and we shook hands. There was no place for me to sit, just child-sized desks. The children's art work and test papers, some marked with gold or silver stars, were tacked on bulletin boards. There was a problem in long division worked out in yellow chalk on the blackboard. I found myself checking the arithmetic.

"You wanted a picture," Lynn London was saying. "I'm afraid I'm not much on family memorabilia. This was the best I could do. This was Barbara in college."

I studied the photo, glanced from it to the woman standing beside me. She caught the eye movement. "If you're looking for a resemblance," she said, "don't waste your time. She looked like our mother."

Lynn favored her father. She had the same chilly blue eyes. Like him she wore glasses, but hers had heavy rims and rectangular lenses. Her brown hair was pulled back and coiled in a tight bun on the back of her head. There was a severity in her face, a sharpness to her features, and although I knew she was only thirty-three she looked several years older. There were lines at the corners of her eyes, deeper ones at the corners of her mouth.

I couldn't get much from Barbara's picture. I'd seen police photos of her after death, high-contrast black and white shot in the kitchen on Wyckoff Street, but I wanted something that would give me a sense of the person and Lynn's photograph didn't supply that, either. I may have been looking for more than a photograph could furnish.

She said, "My father's afraid you'll drag Barbara's name through the mud. Will you?"

"I hadn't planned on it."

"Douglas Ettinger told him something and he's afraid you'll tell it to the world. I wish I knew what it was."

"He told your father that your sister was carrying a black man's child."

"Holy Jesus. Is that true?"

"What do you think?"

"I think Doug's a worm. I've always thought that. Now I know why my father hates you."

"Hates *me?*"

"Uh-huh. I wondered why. In fact I wanted to meet you mostly to find out what kind of man would inspire such a strong reaction in my father. You see, if it weren't for you he wouldn't have been given that piece of information about his sainted daughter. If he hadn't hired you, and if you hadn't talked to Doug—you did talk to Doug, I assume?"

"I met him. At the store in Hicksville."

"If you hadn't, he wouldn't have told my father something my father emphatically did not want to be told. I think he'd prefer to believe that both of his daughters are virgins. Well, he may not care so much about me. I had the temerity to get divorced so that makes me beyond redemption. He'd be sick if I got into an interracial romance, because after all there's a limit, but I don't think

he cares if I have affairs. I'm already damaged goods."
Her voice was flat, less bitter than the words she was
speaking. "But Barbara was a saint. If I got killed he
wouldn't hire you in the first place, but if he did he
wouldn't care what you found. With Barbara it's a different story altogether."

"Was she a saint?"

"We weren't that close." She looked away, picked up
a pencil from the desk top. "She was my big sister. I put
her on a pedestal and wound up seeing her feet of clay,
and I went through a period of holier-than-thou con-
tempt for her. I might have outgrown that but then she
was killed, so I had all that guilt over the way I'd felt
about her." She looked at me. "This is one of the things
I've been working on in therapy."

"Was she having an affair while she was married to
Ettinger?"

"She wouldn't have told me if she had been. The one
thing she did tell me was that he was playing around.
She said he made passes at their friends and that he was
screwing his welfare clients. I don't know if that was true
or not. He never made a pass at me."

She said that last as if it was one more item on a long
list of resentments. I talked with her for another ten minutes and didn't learn anything beyond the fact that Barbara Ettinger's death had had an impact on her sister's
life, and that wasn't news. I wondered how different
Lynn had been nine years ago, and how different she
might have turned out if Barbara had lived. Perhaps it
was all there already, all locked in place, the bitterness,
the emotional armor. I wondered—although I could
probably have guessed—what Lynn's own marriage had
been like. Would she have married the same man if Bar-

bara had been alive? Would she have divorced him if she did?

I left there with a useless photograph and a head full of irrelevant—or unanswerable—questions. I left, too, glad to escape from the woman's cramped personality. Dan Lynch's bar was just a couple blocks uptown, and I turned toward it, remembering the dark wood, the warmth, the boozy, beery aroma.

They were all afraid I'd dig her up, I thought, and it was impossible because she was buried impossibly deep. The bit of poetry Jan had read came to mind and I tried to recall just how it went. *Deep with the first dead*—was that right?

I decided I wanted the exact wording. More than that, I wanted the whole poem. I had a vague recollection of a branch library somewhere around there on Second Avenue. I walked a block north, didn't find it, turned around and walked downtown. There was indeed a library, right where I'd remembered it, a squarish three-story building with a nicely ornamented marble facade. A sign in the door gave the hours, and they were closed on Wednesdays.

All of the branch libraries have cut back on their hours, added closed days. Part of the financial pinch. The city can't afford anything, and the administration goes around like an old miser closing off unused rooms in a sprawling unheated house. The police force is ten thousand men below what it used to be. Everything drops but the rents and the crime rate.

I walked another block and hit St. Marks Place and knew there'd be a bookstore around, and one that would most likely have a poetry section. The busiest commercial block of St. Marks Place, and as trendy a block as the East

Village possesses, runs between Second and Third Avenues. I turned right and walked toward Third, and two-thirds of the way down the block I found a bookstore. They had a paperback edition of the collected poems of Dylan Thomas. I had to go through it a couple of times before I spotted the poem I was looking for, but it was there and I read it all the way through. "A Refusal to Mourn the Death by Fire of a Child in London" was the title. There were parts I didn't think I understood, but I liked the sound of them anyway, the weight and shape of the words.

The poem was long enough to discourage me from trying to copy it into my notebook. Besides, maybe I'd want to look at some of the other poems. I paid for the book and slipped it into my pocket.

Funny how little things nudge you in one direction or another. I had tired myself with all the walking I'd done. I wanted to catch a subway home, but I also wanted a drink and I stood for a moment on the sidewalk in front of the bookstore, trying to decide what to do and where to go. While I was standing there, two patrolmen walked by in uniform. Both of them looked impossibly young, and one was so fresh-faced his uniform looked like a costume.

Across the street, a shop sign read "Haberman's." I don't know what they sold there.

I thought of Burton Havermeyer. I might have thought of him without having seen the cop or having my memory jostled by a name not unlike his. In any event I thought of him, and remembered that he had once lived on this street, that his wife still lived here. I couldn't remember the address, but it was still in my notebook. 212 St. Marks Place, along with the telephone number.

There was still no reason to go look at the building she lived in. He wasn't even part of the case I was working on, because my meeting with Louis Pinell had satisfied me that the little psychopath had killed Susan Potowski and had not killed Barbara Ettinger. But Havermeyer's life had been changed, and in a way that interested me, a way not unlike that in which mine had been changed by another death.

St. Marks Place starts at Third Avenue and the numbers get higher as you go eastward. The block between Second and First was more residential and less commercial. A couple of the row houses had ornate windows and letterboards near the entrance to indicate that they were churches. There was a Ukrainian church, a Polish Catholic church.

I walked to First Avenue, waited for the light, walked on across. I made my way down a quiet block, its houses less prepossessing and in poorer repair than on the preceding block. One of a group of parked cars I passed was a derelict, stripped of tires and hubcaps, the radio pulled out, the interior gutted. On the other side of the street three bearded and longhaired men in Hell's Angels colors were trying to get a motorcycle started.

The last number on the block was 132. The street dead-ended at the corner, where Avenue A formed the western boundary of Tompkins Square Park. I stood there looking at the house number, then at the park, first at one and then at the other.

From Avenue A east to the river are the blocks they call Alphabet City. The population runs to junkies and

muggers and crazies. Nobody decent lives there on purpose, not if they can afford to live anywhere else.

I dragged out my notebook. The address was still the
same, 212 St. Marks Place.

I walked through Tompkins Square and across Avenue B. On my way through the park, drug dealers offered to sell me dope and pills and acid. Either I didn't
look like a cop to them or they just didn't care.

On the other side of Avenue B, the numbers started at
300. And the street signs didn't call it St. Marks Place. It
was East Eighth Street there.

I went back through the park again. At 130 St. Marks
Place there was a bar called Blanche's Tavern. I went in.
The place was a broken-down bucket of blood that
smelled of stale beer and stale urine and bodies that
needed washing. Perhaps a dozen of the bodies were
there, most of them at the bar, a couple at tables. The
place went dead silent when I walked into it. I guess I
didn't look as though I belonged there, and I hope to God
I never do.

I used the phone book first. The precinct in Sheepshead Bay could have made a mistake, or Antonelli could
have read the number to me wrong, or I could have copied it incorrectly. I found him listed, Burton Havermeyer
on West 103rd, but I didn't find any Havermeyers listed
on St. Marks Place.

I was out of dimes. The bartender gave me change.
His customers seemed more relaxed now that they realized I had no business with them.

I dropped a dime in the slot, dialed the number in my
book. No answer.

I went out and walked a few doors to 112 St. Marks
Place. I checked the mail boxes in the vestibule, not really

expecting to find the name Havermeyer, then went back outside. I wanted a drink but Blanche's wasn't where I wanted to have it.

Any port in a storm. I had a straight shot of bourbon at the bar, a top-shelf brand. To my right, two men were discussing some mutual friends. "I told her not to go home with him," one of them was saying. "I told her he was no good and he'd beat her up and rip her off, and she went anyhow, took him on home, and he beat her up and ripped her off. So where's she get off coming and crying to me?"

I tried the number again. On the fourth ring a boy answered it. I thought I'd misdialed, asked if I had the Havermeyer residence. He told me I did.

I asked if Mrs. Havermeyer was there.

"She's next door," he said. "Is it important? Because I could get her."

"Don't bother. I have to check the address for a delivery. What's the house number there?"

"Two twelve."

"Two twelve what?"

He started to tell me the apartment number. I told him I needed to know the name of the street.

"Two twelve St. Marks Place," he said.

I had a moment of the sort I have had now and then in dreams, where the sleeping mind confronts an impossible inconsistency and breaks through to the realization that it is dreaming. Here I was talking to some fresh-voiced child who insisted he lived at an address that did not exist.

Or perhaps he and his mother lived in Tompkins Square Park, with the squirrels.

I said, "What's that between?"

"Huh?"

"What are the cross streets? What block are you on?"

"Oh," he said. "Third and Fourth."

"What?"

"We're between Third and Fourth Avenues."

"That's impossible," I said.

"Huh?"

I looked away from the phone, half-expecting to see something entirely different from the interior of Blanche's Tavern. A lunar landscape, perhaps. St. Marks Place started at Third Avenue and ran east. There was no St. Marks Place between Third and Fourth Avenues.

I said, "Where?"

"Huh? Look, mister, I don't—"

"Wait a minute."

"Maybe I should get my mother. I—"

"What borough?"

"Huh?"

"Are you in Manhattan? Brooklyn? The Bronx? Where are you, son?"

"Brooklyn."

"Are you sure?"

"Yes, I'm sure." He sounded close to tears. "We live in Brooklyn. What do you want, anyway? What's the matter, are you crazy or something?"

"It's all right," I said. "You've been a big help. Thanks a lot."

I hung up, feeling like an idiot. Street names repeated through the five boroughs. I'd had no grounds to assume she lived in Manhattan.

I thought back, replayed what I could of my earlier conversation with the woman. If anything, I might have known that she didn't live in Manhattan. "He's in Manhattan," she had said of her husband. She wouldn't have put it that way if she'd been in Manhattan herself.

But what about my conversation with Havermeyer? "You're wife's still in the East Village," I'd said, and he'd agreed with me.

Well, maybe he'd just wanted the conversation to end. It was easier to agree with me than to explain that there was another St. Marks Place in Brooklyn.

Still . . .

I left Blanche's and hurried west to the bookstore where I'd bought the book of poems. They had a Hagstrom pocket atlas of the five boroughs. I looked up St. Marks Place in the back, turned to the appropriate map, found what I was looking for.

St. Marks Place, in Brooklyn as in Manhattan, extends for only three blocks. To the east, across Flatbush Avenue, the same street continues at an angle as St. Marks Avenue, stretching under that name clear to Brownsville.

To the west, St. Marks Place stops at Third Avenue— just as it does at an altogether different Third Avenue in Manhattan. On the other side of Third, Brooklyn's St. Marks Place has another name.

Wyckoff Street.

SIXTEEN

It must have been around three o'clock when I spoke with the boy. It was between six-thirty and seven by the time I mounted the stoop of his building on West 103rd. I'd found things to do during the intervening hours.

I rang a couple of bells but not his, and someone buzzed me in. Whoever it was peered at me from a doorway on the third floor but didn't challenge my right to pass. I stood at Havermeyer's door and listened for a moment. The television was on, turned to the local news.

I didn't really expect him to shoot through the door but he did wear a gun as a security guard, and although he probably left it in the store each night I couldn't be sure he didn't have another one at home. They teach you to stand at the side of a door when you knock on it, so I did. I heard his footsteps approach the door, then his voice asking who it was.

"Scudder," I said.

He opened the door. He was in street clothes and probably left not only the gun but the entire uniform at the store each night. He had a can of beer in one hand. I asked if I could come in. His reaction time was slow but at length he nodded and made room for me. I entered and drew the door shut.

He said, "Still on that case, huh? Something I can do for you?"

"Yes."

"Well, I'll be glad to help if I can. Meantime, how about a beer?"

I shook my head. He looked at the can of beer he was holding, moved to set it down on a table, went over and turned off the television set. He held the pose for a moment and I studied his face in profile. He didn't need a shave this time. He turned slowly, expectantly, as if waiting for the blow to fall.

I said, "I know you killed her, Burt."

I watched his deep brown eyes. He was rehearsing his denial, running it through his mind, and then there was a moment when he decided not to bother. Something went out of him.

"When did you know?"

"A couple of hours ago."

"When you left here Sunday I couldn't figure whether you knew or not. I thought maybe you were going cat-and-mouse with me. But I didn't get that feeling. I felt close to you, actually. I felt we were a couple of ex-cops, two guys who left the force for personal reasons. I thought maybe you were playing a part, setting a trap, but it didn't feel like it."

"I wasn't."

"How did you find out?"

"St. Marks Place. You didn't live in the East Village after all. You lived in Brooklyn three blocks away from Barbara Ettinger."

"Thousands of people lived that close to her."

"You let me go on thinking you lived in the East Village. I don't know if I'd have had a second thought about it if I'd known from the beginning that you had lived in Brooklyn. Maybe I would have. But most likely I wouldn't. Brooklyn's a big place. I didn't know there was a St. Marks Place in it so I certainly didn't know where it was in relation to Wyckoff Street. For all I knew, it could have been out in Sheepshead Bay near your precinct. But you lied about it."

"Just to avoid getting into a long explanation. It doesn't prove anything."

"It gave me a reason to take a look at you. And the first thing I took a look at was another lie you told me. You said you and your wife didn't have any kids. But I talked to your boy on the phone this afternoon, and I called back and asked him his father's name and how old he was. He must have wondered what I was doing asking him all those questions. He's twelve. He was three years old when Barbara Ettinger was killed."

"So?"

"You used to take him to a place on Clinton Street. The Happy Hours Child Care Center."

"You're guessing."

"No."

"They're out of business. They've been out of business for years."

"They were still in business when you left Brooklyn. Did you keep tabs on the place?"

"My ex-wife must have mentioned it," he said. Then he shrugged. "Maybe I walked past there once. When I was in Brooklyn visiting Danny."

"The woman who ran the day-care center is living in New York. She'll remember you."

"After nine years?"

"That's what she says. And she kept records, Burt. The ledgers with the names and addresses of students and their parents, along with the record of payments. She packed all that stuff in a carton when she closed the business and never bothered to go through it and throw out the things she didn't need to keep anymore. She opened the box today. She says she remembers you. You always brought the boy, she said. She never met your wife but she does remember you."

"She must have a good memory."

"You were usually in uniform. That's an easy thing to remember."

He looked at me for a moment, then turned and walked over to the window and stood looking out of it. I don't suppose he was looking at anything in particular.

"Where'd you get the icepick, Burt?"

Without turning he said, "I don't have to admit to anything. I don't have to answer any questions."

"Of course you don't."

"Even if you were a cop I wouldn't have to say any-thing. And you're not a cop. You've got no authority."

"You're absolutely right."

"So why should I answer your questions?"

"You've been sitting on it a long time, Burt."

"So?"

"Doesn't it get to you a little? Keeping it inside all that time?"

"Oh, God," he said. He went over to a chair, dropped into it. "Bring me that beer," he said. "Could you do that for me?"

I gave it to him. He asked me if I was sure I didn't want one for myself. No thanks, I said. He drank some beer and I asked him where he got the icepick.

"Some store," he said. "I don't remember."

"In the neighborhood?"

"I think in Sheepshead Bay. I'm not sure."

"You knew Barbara Ettinger from the day-care center."

"And from the neighborhood. I used to see her around the neighborhood before I started taking Danny to the center."

"And you were having an affair with her?"

"Who told you that? No, I wasn't having an affair with her. I wasn't having an affair with anybody."

"But you wanted to."

"No."

I waited but he seemed willing to leave it there. I said, "Why did you kill her, Burt?"

He looked at me for a moment, then looked down, then looked at me again. "You can't prove anything," he said.

I shrugged.

"You can't. And I don't have to tell you anything." A deep breath, a long sigh. "Something happened when I saw the Potowski woman," he said. "Something happened."

"What do you mean?"

"Something happened to *me*. Inside of me. Something came into my head and I couldn't get rid of it. I remember standing and hitting myself in the forehead but I couldn't get it out of my mind."

"You wanted to kill Barbara Ettinger."

"No. Don't help me out, okay? Let me find the words by myself."

"I'm sorry."

"I looked at the dead woman and it wasn't her I saw on the floor, it was my wife. Every time the picture came back to me, the murder scene, the woman on the floor, I saw my wife in the picture. And I couldn't get it out of my head to kill her that way."

He took a little sip of beer. Over the top of the can he said, "I used to think about killing her. Plenty of times I thought that it was the only way out. I couldn't stand being married. I was alone, my parents were dead, I never had any brothers or sisters, and I thought I needed somebody. Besides, I knew she needed me. But it was wrong. I hated being married. It was around my neck like a collar that's too small for you, it was choking me and I couldn't get out of it."

"Why couldn't you just leave her?"

"How could I leave her? How could I do that to her? What kind of a man leaves a woman like that?"

"Men leave women every day."

"You don't understand, do you?" Another sigh. "Where was I? Yeah. I used to think about killing her. I would think about it, and I would think, sure, and the first thing they'd do is check you inside and out, and one way or another they'll hang it on you, because they always go to the husband first and ninety percent of the time that's who did it, and they'll break your story down and break you down and where does that leave you? But then I saw the Potowski woman and it was all there. I

could kill her and make it look like the Icepick Prowler
had one more on his string. I saw what we did with the
Potowski killing. We just bucked it to Manhattan South,
we didn't hassle the husband or anything like that."

"So you decided to kill her."

"Right."

"Your wife."

"Right."

"Then how does Barbara Ettinger come into this?"

"Oh, God," he said.

I waited him out.

"I was afraid to kill her. My wife, I mean. I was afraid
something would go wrong. I thought, suppose I start
and I can't go through with it? I had the icepick and I
would take it out and look at it and—I remember now, I
bought it on Atlantic Avenue. I don't even know if the
store's still there."

"It doesn't matter."

"I know. I had visions of, you know, starting to stab
her and stopping, of not being able to finish the job, and
the things that were going through my mind were driving me crazy. I guess I *was* crazy. Of course I was."

He drank from the beer can. "I killed her for practice,"
he said.

"Barbara Ettinger."

"Yes. I had to find out if I could do it. And I told myself it would be a precaution. One more icepick killing in
Brooklyn, so that when my wife got murdered three
blocks away it would be just one more in the string. And
it would be the same. Maybe no matter how I did it
they'd notice a difference between it and the real icepick
killings, but they would never have a reason to suspect
me of killing some stranger like the Ettinger woman, and

then my wife would be killed the same way, and—but that was just what I was telling myself. I killed her because I was afraid to kill my wife and I had to kill someone."

"You had to kill someone?"

"I *had* to." He leaned forward, sat on the edge of his chair. "I couldn't get it out of my mind. Do you know what it's like when you can't get something out of your mind?"

"Yes."

"I couldn't think who to pick. And then one day I took Danny to the day-care center and she and I talked the way we always did, and the idea came to me. I thought of killing her and the thought fit."

"What do you mean, the thought fit?"

"She belonged in the picture. I could see her, you know, on the kitchen floor. So I started watching her. When I wasn't working I would hang around the neighborhood and keep tabs on her."

She had sensed that someone was following her, watching her. And she'd been afraid, ever since the Potowski murder, that someone was stalking her.

"And I decided it would be all right to kill her. She didn't have any children. Nobody was dependent upon her. And she was immoral. She flirted with me, she flirted with men at the day-care center. She had men to her apartment when her husband was out. I thought, if I screwed it up and they knew it wasn't the Icepick Prowler, there would be plenty of other suspects. They'd never get to me."

I asked him about the day of the murder.

"My shift ended around noon that day. I went over to Clinton Street and sat in a coffee shop at the counter where I could keep an eye on the place. When she left early I followed her. I was across the street watching her building when a man went into it. I knew him, I'd seen him with her before."

"Was he black?"

"Black? No. Why?"

"No reason."

"I don't remember what he looked like. He was with her for a half-hour or so. Then he left. I waited a little while longer, and something told me, I don't know, I just knew this was the right time. I went up and knocked on her door."

"And she let you in?"

"I showed her my shield. And I reminded her that she knew me from the day-care center, that I was Danny's father. She let me in."

"And?"

"I don't want to talk about it."

"Are you sure of that?"

I guess he thought it over. Then he said, "We were in the kitchen. She was making me a cup of coffee, she had her back to me, and I put one hand over her mouth and jabbed the icepick into her chest. I wanted to get her heart right away, I didn't want her to suffer. I kept stabbing her in the heart and she collapsed in my arms and I let her fall to the floor." He raised his liquid brown eyes to mine. "I think she was dead right then," he said. "I think she died right away."

"And you went on stabbing her."

"When I thought about it before I did it, I always went crazy and stabbed over and over like a maniac. I had that picture in my mind, but I couldn't do it that way. I had to make myself stab her and I was sick, I thought I was going to throw up, and I had to keep on sticking that icepick into her body and—" He broke off, gasping for breath. His face was drawn and his pale complexion was ghostly.

"It's all right," I said.

"Oh, God."

"Take it easy, Burt."

"God, God."

"You only stabbed one of her eyes."

"It was so *hard*," he said. "Her eyes were wide open. I knew she was dead, I knew she couldn't see anything, but those eyes were just staring at me. I had the hardest time making myself stab her in the eye. I did it once and then I just couldn't do it again. I tried but I just couldn't do it again."

"And then?"

"I left. No one saw me leave. I just left the building and walked away. I put the icepick down a sewer. I thought, I did it, I killed her and I got away with it, but I didn't feel as though I got away with anything. I felt sick to my stomach. I thought about what I had done and I couldn't believe I'd really done it. When the story was on television and in the papers I couldn't believe it. I thought that someone else must have done it."

"And you didn't kill your wife."

He shook his head. "I knew I could never do something like that again. You know something? I've thought about all of it, over and over, and I think I was out of my mind. In fact I'm sure of it. Something about seeing Mrs. Potowski, those pools of blood in her eyes, those stab wounds all over her body, it did something to me. It made me crazy, and I went on being crazy until Barbara

Ettinger was dead. Then I was all right again, but she was dead.

"All of a sudden certain things were clear. I couldn't stay married anymore, and for the first time I realized I didn't have to. I could leave my wife and Danny. I had thought that would be a horrible thing to do, but here I'd been planning on killing her, and now I'd actually killed somebody and I knew how much more horrible that was than anything else I could possibly do to her, like leaving."

I led him through it again, went over a few points. He finished his beer but didn't get another. I wanted a drink, but I didn't want beer and I didn't want to drink with him. I didn't hate him. I don't know exactly what I felt for him. But I didn't want to drink with him.

He broke a silence to say, "Nobody can prove any of this. It doesn't matter what I told you. There are no witnesses and there's no evidence."

"People could have seen you in the neighborhood."

"And still remember nine years later? And remember what day it was?"

He was right, of course. I couldn't imagine a District Attorney who'd even try for an indictment. There was nothing to make a case out of.

1 said, "Why don't you put a coat on, Burt."

"What for?"

"We'll go down to the Thirteenth Precinct and talk to a cop named Fitzroy. You can tell him what you told me."

"That'd be pretty stupid, wouldn't it?"

"Why?"

"All I have to do is keep on the way I've been. All I have to do is keep my mouth shut. Nobody can prove anything. They couldn't even try to prove anything."

"That's probably true."

"And you want me to confess."

"That's right."

His expression was childlike. "Why?"

To tie off the ends, I thought. To make it neat. To show Frank Fitzroy that he was right when he said I just might solve the case.

What I said was, "You'll feel better."

"That's a laugh."

"How do you feel now, Burt?"

"How do I feel?" He considered the question. Then, as if surprised by his answer, "I feel okay."

"Better than when I got here?"

"Yeah."

"Better than you've felt since Sunday?"

"I suppose so."

"You never told anybody, did you?"

"Of course not."

"Not a single person in nine years. You probably didn't think about it much, but there were times when you couldn't help thinking about it, and you never told anybody."

"So?"

"That's a long time to carry it."

"God."

"I don't know what they'll do with you, Burt. You may not do any time. Once I talked a murderer into killing himself, and he did it, and I wouldn't do that again. And another time I talked a murderer into confessing because I convinced him he would probably kill himself if he didn't confess first. I don't think you'd do that. I think you've lived with this for nine years and maybe you could go on living with it. But do you really want to? Wouldn't you rather let go of it?"

"God," he said. He put his head in his hands. "I'm all mixed up," he said.

"You'll be all right."

"They'll put my picture in the papers. It'll be on the news. What's that going to make it like for Danny?"

"You've got to worry about yourself first."

"I'll lose my job," he said. "What'll happen to me?"

I didn't answer that one. I didn't have an answer.

"Okay," he said suddenly.

"Ready to go?"

"I guess."

On the way downtown he said, "I think I knew Sunday. I knew you'd keep poking at it until you found out I did it. I had an urge to tell you right then."

"I got lucky. A couple of coincidences put me on St. Marks Place and I thought of you and had nothing better to do than see the house where you used to live. But the numbers stopped at One-three-two."

"If it wasn't that coincidence there would have been another one. It was all set from the minute you walked into my apartment. Maybe earlier than that. Maybe it was a sure thing from the minute I killed her. Some people get away with murder but I guess I'm not one of them."

"Nobody gets away with it. Some people just don't get caught."

"Isn't that the same thing?"

"'You didn't get caught for nine years, Burt. What were you getting away with?"

"Oh," he said. "I get it."

And just before we got to the One-Three I said, "There's something I don't understand. Why did you think it would be easier to kill your wife than to leave her? You said several times that it would be such a terrible thing to leave a woman like her, that it would be a contemptible act, but men and women leave each other all the time. You couldn't have been worried about what your parents would think because you didn't have any family left. What made it such a big deal?"

"Oh," he said. "You don't know."

"Don't know what?"

"You haven't met her. You didn't go out there this afternoon, did you?"

"No."

(*"I never see him ... I never see my former husband ... I don't see my husband and I don't see the check. Do you see? Do you?"*)

"The Potowski woman, with her eyes staring up through the blood. When I saw her like that it just hit me so hard I couldn't deal with it. But you wouldn't understand that because you don't know about her."

(*"Perhaps he has a phone and perhaps it's in the book. You could look it up. I know you'll excuse me if I don't offer to look it up for you."*)

The answer was floating out there. I could very nearly reach out and touch it. But my mind wouldn't fasten onto it.

He said, "My wife is blind."

SEVENTEEN

It turned out to be a long night, although the trip to Twentieth Street was the least of it. I shared a cab down with Burton Havermeyer. We must have talked about something en route but I can't remember what. I paid for the cab, took Havermeyer to the squad room and introduced him to Frank Fitzroy, and that was pretty much the extent of my contribution. I, after all, was not the arresting officer. I had no official connection with the case and had performed no official function. I didn't have to be around while a stenographer took down Havermeyer's statement, nor was I called upon to make a statement of my own.

Fitzroy slipped away long enough to walk me down to the corner and buy me a drink at P. J. Reynolds.

I didn't much want to accept his invitation. I wanted a drink, but I wasn't much more inclined to drink with him than with Havermeyer. I felt closed off from everyone, locked up tight within myself where dead women and blind women couldn't get at me.

The drinks came and we drank them, and he said, "Nice piece of work, Matt."

"I got lucky."

"You don't get that kind of luck. You make it. Something put you onto Havermeyer in the first place."

"More luck. The other two cops from the Six-One were dead. He was odd man in."

"You could have talked to him on the phone. Something made you go see him."

"Lack of anything better to do."

"And then you asked him enough questions so that he told a couple of lies that could catch him up further down the line."

"And I was in the right place at the right time, and the right shop sign caught my eye when the right pair of cops walked in front of me."

"Oh, shit," he said, and signaled the bartender. "Put yourself down if you want."

"I just don't think I did anything to earn a field promotion to Chief of Detectives. That's all."

The bartender came around. Fitzroy pointed to our glasses and the bartender filled them up again. I let him pay for this round, as he had paid for the first one.

He said, "You won't get any official recognition out of this, Matt. You know that, don't you?"

"I'd prefer it that way."

"What we'll tell the press is the reopening of the case with the arrest of Pinell made him conscience-stricken, and he turned himself in. He talked it over with you, another ex-cop like himself, and decided to confess. How does that sound?"

"It sounds like the truth."

"Just a few things left out is all. What I was saying, you won't get anything official out of it, but people around the department are gonna know better. You follow me?"

"So?"

"So you couldn't ask for a better passport back onto the force is what it sounds like to me. I was talking to Eddie Koehler over at the Sixth. You wouldn't have any trouble getting 'em to take you on again."

"It's not what I want."

"That's what he said you'd say. But are you sure it isn't? All right, you're a loner, you got a hard-on for the world, you hit this stuff—" he touched his glass "—a little harder than you maybe should. But you're a cop, Matt, and you didn't stop being one when you gave the badge back."

I thought for a moment, not to consider his proposal but to weigh the words of my reply. I said, "You're right, in a way. But in another way you're wrong, and I stopped being a cop *before* I handed in my shield."

"All because of that kid that died."

"Not just that." I shrugged. "People move and their lives change."

"Well," he said, and then he didn't say anything for a few minutes, and then we found something less unsettling to talk about. We discussed the impossibility of keeping three-card monte dealers off the street, given that the fine for the offense is seventy-five dollars and the profit somewhere between five hundred and a thousand dollars a day. "And there's this one judge," he said, "who told a whole string of them he'd let 'em off without a fine if they'd promise not to do it again. 'Oh, Ah promises, yo honor.' To save seventy-five dollars, those assholes'd promise to grow hair on their tongues."

We had a third round of drinks, and I let him pay for that round, too, and then he went back to the station house and I caught a cab home. I checked the desk for messages, and when there weren't any I went around the corner to Armstrong's, and that's where it got to be a long night.

But it wasn't a bad one. I drank my bourbon in coffee, sipping it, making it last, and my mood didn't turn black or ugly. I talked to people intermittently but spent a lot of time replaying the day, listening to Havermeyer's explanation. Somewhere in the course of things I gave Jan a call to tell her how things had turned out. Her line was busy. Either she was talking to someone or she had the phone off the hook, and this time I didn't get the operator to find out which.

I had just the right amount to drink, for a change. Not so much that I blacked out and lost my memory. But enough to bring sleep without dreams.

By the time I got down to Pine Street the next day, Charles London knew what to expect. The morning papers had the story. The line they carried was pretty much what I'd expected from what Fitzroy had said. I was mentioned by name as the fellow ex-cop who'd heard Havermeyer's confession and escorted him in so he could give himself up for the murder of Barbara Ettinger.

Even so, he didn't look thrilled to see me.

"I owe you an apology," he said. "I managed to become convinced that your investigation would only have a damaging effect upon a variety of people. I thought—"

"I know what you thought."

"It turned out that I was wrong. I'm still concerned about what might come out in a trial, but it doesn't look as though there will be a trial."

"You don't have to worry about what comes out anyway," I said. "Your daughter wasn't carrying a black baby." He looked as though he'd been slapped. "She was carrying her husband's baby. She may very well have been having an affair, probably in retaliation for her husband's behavior, but there's no evidence that it had an interracial element. That was an invention of your former son-in-law's."

"I see." He took his little walk to the window and made sure that the harbor was still out there. He turned to me and said, "At least this has turned out well, Mr. Scudder."

"Oh?"

"Barbara's killer has been brought to justice. I no longer have to worry who might have killed her, or why. Yes, I think we can say it's turned out well."

He could say it if he wanted. I wasn't sure that justice was what Burton Havermeyer had been brought to, or where his life would go from here. I wasn't sure where justice figured in the ordeal that was just beginning for Havermeyer's son and his blind ex-wife. And if London didn't have to worry that Douglas Ettinger had killed his daughter, what he'd learned about Ettinger's character couldn't have been monumentally reassuring.

I thought, too, of the fault lines I'd already detected in Ettinger's second marriage. I wondered how long the blonde with the sunny suburban face would hold her space in his desk-top cube. If they split, would he be able to go on working for his second father-in-law?

Finally, I thought how people could adjust to one reality after another if they put their minds to it. London had begun by believing that his daughter had been killed for no reason at all, and he'd adjusted to that. Then he came to believe that she had indeed been killed for a reason, and by someone who knew her well. And he'd set about adjusting to that. Now he knew that she'd been killed by a near-stranger for a reason that had nothing much to do with her. Her death had come in a dress rehearsal for murder, and in dying she'd preserved the life of the intended victim. You could see all that as part of some great design or you could see it as further proof that the world was mad, but either way it was a new reality to which he would surely adjust.

Before I left he gave me a check for a thousand dollars. A bonus, he said, and he assured me he wanted me to have it. I gave him no argument. When money comes with no strings on it, you take it and put it in your pocket. I was still enough of a cop at heart to remember that much.

I tried Jan around lunchtime and there was no answer. I tried her again later in the afternoon and the line was busy three times running. It was around six when I finally reached her.

"You're hard to get hold of," I said.

"I was out some. And then I was on the phone."

"I was out some myself." I told her a lot of what had happened since I'd left her loft the previous afternoon, armed with the knowledge that Havermeyer's boy Danny had attended the Happy Hours Child Care Center. I told her why Barbara Ettinger had been killed, and I told her that Havermeyer's wife was blind.

"Jesus," she said.

We talked a little more, and I asked her what she was doing about dinner. "My client gave me a thousand dollars that I didn't do a thing to earn," I said, "and I feel a need to spend some of it frivolously before I piss the rest of it away on necessities."

"I'm afraid tonight's out," she said. "I was just making myself a salad."

"Well, do you want to hit a couple of high spots after you finish your salad? Anyplace but Blanche's Tavern is fine with me."

There was a pause. Then she said, "The thing is, Matthew, I have something on tonight."

"Oh."

"And it's not another date. I'm going to a meeting."

"A meeting?"

"An AA meeting."

"I see."

"I'm an alcoholic, Matthew. I've got to face the fact and I've got to deal with it."

"I didn't have the impression that you drank that much."

"It's not how much you drink. It's what it does to you. I have blackouts. I have personality changes. I tell myself I'm not going to drink and I do. I tell myself I'm going to have one drink and the next morning the bottle's empty. I'm an alcoholic."

"You were in AA before."

"That's right."

"I thought it didn't work for you."

"Oh, it was working fine. Until I drank. This time I want to give it a chance."

I thought for a minute. "Well, I think that's great," I said.

"You do?"

"Yes, I do," I said, and meant it. "I think it's terrific. I know it works for a lot of people and there's no reason why you can't make it work. You're going to a meeting tonight?"

"That's right. I was at one this afternoon."

"I thought they only had them at night."

"They have them all the time, and all over the city."

"How often do you have to go?"

"You don't have to do anything. They recommend ninety meetings in the first ninety days, but you can go to more. I have plenty of time. I can go to a lot of them."

"That's great."

"After the meeting this afternoon I was on the phone with somebody I knew when I was in the program last time. And I'm going to a meeting tonight, and that'll get me through today, and I'll have one day of sobriety."

"Uh-huh."

"That's how it's done, you see. You take it one day at a time."

"That's great." I wiped my forehead. It gets warm in a phone booth with the door closed. "When do those meetings end? Ten or ten-thirty, something like that?"

"Ten o'clock."

"Well, suppose—"

"But people generally go out for coffee afterward."

"Uh-huh. Well, suppose I came by around eleven? Or later, if you figure you'll want to spend more than an hour over coffee."

"I don't think that's a very good idea, Matthew."

"Oh."

"I want to give this a fair shot. I don't want to start sabotaging myself before I even get started."

I said, "Jan? I wasn't planning to come over and drink with you."

"I know that."

"Or in front of you, as far as that goes. I won't drink when I'm with you. That's no problem."

"Because you can stop anytime you want to."

"I can certainly not drink when we're together."

Another pause, and when she spoke I could hear the strain in her voice. "God," she said. "Matthew, darling, it's not quite that simple."

"Oh?"

"One of the things they tell us is that we're powerless over people, places and things."

"I don't know what that means."

"It means to avoid those elements that can increase our desire to drink."

"And I'm one of those elements?"

"I'm afraid so."

I cracked the phone booth door, let a little air in. I said, "Well, what does that mean, exactly? That we never see each other again?"

"Oh, God."

"Just tell me the rules so I'll understand."

"Jesus, God. I can't think in terms of never again. I can't even think in terms of never having a drink again. I'm supposed to take it a day at a time, so let's do this in terms of today."

"You don't want to see me today."

"Of *course* I want to see you today! Oh, Jesus. Look, if you want to come over around eleven—"

"No," I said.

"What?"

"I said no. You were right the first time and I shouldn't be doing a number on you. I'm like my client, that's all. I've just got to adjust to a new reality. I think you're doing the right thing."

"Do you really?"

"Yes. And if I'm somebody you ought to stay away from, I think that's what you'd better do for the time being. And if we're supposed to get together later on, well, it'll happen."

A pause. Then, "Thank you, Matthew."

For what? I got out of the booth and went back upstairs to my room. I put on a clean shirt and tie and treated myself to a good steak dinner at the Slate. It's a hangout for cops from John Jay College and Midtown South, but I was lucky enough not to see anyone that I knew. I had a big meal all by myself, with a martini in front and a brandy afterward.

I walked back to Ninth Avenue and passed St. Paul's. The church itself was closed now. I descended a narrow flight of steps to the basement. Not the big room in front where they have Bingo a couple nights a week, but a smaller room on the side where they have the meetings.

When you live in a neighborhood you know where different things are. Whether you have any interest in them or not.

I stood in front of the door for a minute or two. I felt a little lightheaded, a little congested in the chest. I decided that was probably from the brandy. It's a powerful stimulant. I'm not used to it, don't drink it often.

I opened the door and looked in. A couple dozen people sitting in folding chairs. A table holding a big coffee urn and a few stacks of Styrofoam cups. Some slogans taped to the wall—EASY DOES IT, KEEP IT SIMPLE. The fucking wisdom of the ages.

She was probably in a room like this downtown. Some church basement in SoHo, say.

Best of luck, lady.

I stepped back, let the door shut, walked up the stairs. I had visions of the door opening behind me, people chasing after me and dragging me back. Nothing like that happened.

The tight feeling was still there in my chest.

The brandy, I told myself. Probably be a good idea to stay away from it. Stick to what you're used to. Stick to bourbon.

I went on over to Armstrong's. A little bourbon would take the edge off the brandy rush. A little bourbon would take the edge off almost anything.

THE END

LAWRENCE BLOCK

Lawrence Block is a Grandmaster of the Mystery Writers of America, and has won a total of fourteen awards for his fiction, including one Edgar Award and two Shamus Awards for best novels for titles in the Matt Scudder series. He is also the creator of other great characters such as Bernie Rhodenbarr, Evan Tanner and Chip Harrison, and has written dozens of award-winning short stories. Lawrence Block lives in New York City.

EMAIL: lawbloc@gmail.com
BLOG: http://lawrenceblock.wordpress.com
FACEBOOK: http://www.facebook.com/lawrence.block
WEBSITE: http://www.lawrenceblock.com
TWITTER: @LawrenceBlock

CPSIA information can be obtained at www.ICGtesting.com
Printed in the USA
LVOW081822080113

314889LV00004B/514/P